SANTA'S ANGELS

SANTA'S ANGELS

•

Janet Kaderli

AVALON BOOKS

NEW YORK

Published by Thomas Bouregy & Co., Inc.
160 Madison Avenue, New York, NY 10016

Library of Congress Cataloging-in-Publication Data

Kaderli, Janet.
    Santa's angels / Janet Kaderli.
        p. cm.
    ISBN 978-0-8034-9925-6 (acid-free paper)
    1. Christmas stories.   I. Title.
    PS3611.A327S26 2008
    813'.6—dc22

                        2008023177

PRINTED IN THE UNITED STATES OF AMERICA
ON ACID-FREE PAPER
BY HADDON CRAFTSMEN, BLOOMSBURG, PENNSYLVANIA

For everyone who loves Christmas
and happily ever after

Chapter One

Now *those* were well-filled stockings.

Santa let his thoughts wander while he watched Elf Janie corral a runaway toddler. Being a department store Santa was a tedious job. Acting kind and jolly all day with babies crying and toddlers refusing to smile for their picture had never been part of his game plan. But this shift he was working with Elf Janie was almost enjoyable. Janie wasn't like most women he knew. But then he didn't dress like Santa when he was around those women.

Or behave all kind and jolly.

He managed a smile as Janie deposited a kid—damp on both ends—in his lap.

"Thank you, Elf Janie," he said, then turned to the boy in his lap. "Ho ho ho, what do you want for Christmas?"

In response the youngster stuck out his bottom lip and did a great imitation of someone who was deaf and mute.

A woman pleaded from the sidelines, "Come on, Joey, give Santa a smile so we'll have a nice picture to send to Grandma."

Joey sat like a rock.

"Say, Joey, do you like chocolate kisses or candy canes?" Elf Janie asked from behind the camera.

"Can'y canes!" Joey exclaimed, tricked into smiling for the split second it took Janie to snap a picture.

Field goal, Santa thought, approving Janie's strategy. *If you can't make a touchdown, go for three.*

"Next!"

Santa sighed as he looked at the line—never-ending on this day after Thanksgiving. For most of the next month, he'd have to put on this getup and lay low until all the adverse publicity surrounding his last escapade died down.

Playing Santa had seemed like a godsend when his uncle, Nicodemus "Fil" Filmore, the CEO of Filmore's Department Stores, had offered him the job. It provided the gainful employment his probation demanded as well as a disguise for his too well-known face. The whole thing had seemed like a joke: Nick Klaus, the selfish, inconsiderate football player turned sports announcer as wise, generous St. Nick. He hadn't counted on being poked and prodded by tiny elbows and knees; being wet on, cried on, and never being able to frown.

So here he was, in his uncle's main department store, enthroned in a decorator's vision of toyland, with a five-year-old rugrat on his lap. The only thing the least bit fun about the situation was working with Elf Janie. He gave her a smile just as she snapped a picture for some grandma's brag book.

The hours dragged inexorably to closing time. As the last kid was carried off by his mother, Santa stood and stretched his bum knee.

"It's been a long day, Elf Janie," he said, taking a naughty sense of pleasure in trying to provoke her.

"It sure has," she agreed, not even giving him a dirty look.

Must be tired. He sure was. His back and shoulders ached with stiffness from sitting so long. Even his cheeks hurt from smiling. Maybe hers did too. The cheerful, friendly expression she'd worn all day around the kids was long gone.

"Just twenty-seven more shopping days 'til Christmas," he reminded her, hoping to start a conversation as she packed away the camera equipment. He was so bored with his own company, soon he'd start talking to the oversized stuffed animals guarding the entrance to Santa-Land.

"Bah, humbug," she muttered.

"Hey, what's this? Elf Janie in a bad mood?" He tried the ho-ho-ho voice he used with the kids with pretty much the same results. No response, not even a smile. "I figured you'd be whistling Christmas songs while you run your errands, like here in Santa-Land."

Turning from her work, she looked him straight in

the eye, all friendliness gone from her expression. "Yeah, well, Santa–Land's not the real world, is it?" Pushing past him, she started for the employee lounge.

"What's the problem?" he asked, falling into step with her as they walked down the aisles decorated with swags of artificial pine and large red bows. The door to the employee lounge was half-hidden behind a display of potpourri and candles. The spicy scent of pine and cinnamon with a hint of vanilla always made him sneeze when he passed.

"Bless you," Janie said, pushing open the door marked EMPLOYEES ONLY. She went on ahead without a backward glance as he stopped to pull out a handkerchief and rub his nose.

Santa shrugged and went through the door. A short hall led into an open room, with the employee breakroom and restrooms on one side. On the other side, Janie stood at a row of lockers. As she reached into her locker, her purse tumbled out, spilling objects across the floor.

"Need a hand?" he asked, pausing.

"No, thanks, I've got it." She gathered everything up, stuffed it into her purse, then pulled a change of clothes out of her locker.

Store policy demanded that Santa and his helpers never be seen outside the store in their costumes. Santa took the policy one step further by making sure no one working in the store ever saw him *out* of costume. The red cap, angel-hair beard, and bulky costume stayed *on*, covering the brush of auburn hair, square jaw, and muscular physique everyone in the Dallas/Fort Worth Metroplex would recognize. The only other person who knew Nick Klaus, sports anchor from Channel Thirty-two News, played Santa was his uncle. To everyone else he was Santa, plain and simple. Which meant he'd wait here in the lounge until all the other employees left for the evening. Then he'd change in the restroom, leaving his costume to be cleaned for the following day.

Janie wove her way to the restroom, avoiding the other employees who stopped in the breakroom before heading home. Nick noticed how she ignored the other people, as if she was trying to be invisible. As if she could. A pretty girl, sure, with curly dark hair and brown eyes, but there was more to her than just appearances. She had the patience of a saint, for one thing, working all day with little kids and a smile on her face.

But now that smile was gone.

Maybe she had her reasons to try to be invisible. After all, he was in that kind of spot. If the ground had just opened up and swallowed him after the accident—even before the accident—everyone's life would've been better off.

He narrowed his eyes, looking at the closed door as if that would give him X-ray vision, allowing him to see Janie and learn her story. Was she, like him, hiding? What horrendous thing could she have done? Sweet Elf Janie, who made the kids laugh and took such wonderful pictures of them. Shaking his head, he turned away and began searching his pockets for change for the vending machine, knowing he was completely off base. Janie was one of the good ones. Her mistakes, if she made any, were nothing compared to his.

Janie tugged at the zipper that ran down her back. It wouldn't budge. After numerous contortions, including trying to slip the tunic over her head without unzipping it, she gave up.

Great. Now she'd be late for her next job.

She opened the restroom door a crack, which gave her a limited view of the breakroom. No one seemed to be around. *Darn.* She couldn't get this zipper undone without help. Maybe someone was still in the breakroom or the locker room. Slipping out of the restroom, she froze when she saw a red-suited man plunking change into the drink machine, whistling "Santa Claus Is Coming to Town."

Santa.

She hesitated. Should she ask Santa for help or look for someone else? She worked with two Santas, and this wasn't the one she'd choose to ask for help. He made her uncomfortable with his teasing and those great-looking green eyes that followed her constantly. His height made her feel like she actually was an elf, especially when he walked beside her as he had today. And that wasn't all padding under his suit but pure muscle. He lifted kids on and off his lap like they were weightless.

Janie sighed and walked toward him. Better to let Santa unzip her than be late.

"Santa?" she called, feeling stupid that she didn't even know his real name.

"Yo!" He swung around, causing her to step back. He was so tall, his shoulders so broad. The red costume made him seem larger than life, and, for a moment, she couldn't speak.

"Can I help you, Elf Janie?" he asked, the corners of his eyes crinkling as he smiled at her.

"Could you give me a hand? My zipper's stuck and—"

"Sure thing." Santa strode up to her without hesitation. Disconcerted, Janie stood gazing up at him. He took her by the shoulders and gently turned her until she faced away from him.

"The zipper's in back, right? Yeah, I can see where it's caught. Just a second, now—don't want to tear your dress."

Cool air chilled the skin that was bared as the zipper slowly tracked down her back. Surely, it didn't take that long to unzip a dress? As soon as she felt the zipper reach her waist, she stepped away.

"Thanks," she said, glancing over her shoulder as she moved away.

"Anytime," he answered, his eyes crinkling again as if he enjoyed her discomfort.

Janie hurried back to the restroom, threw on the short black skirt and white knit top that was the uniform for her next job, and charged out the employees' entrance.

On her way to her late-night job, she switched on the radio to her favorite classic rock station. She sang along with the songs, turning up the volume, acclimating herself to the atmosphere of her next job as she drove from downtown Dallas out Gaston Avenue.

Although not physically far apart, the Happy Honcho was as far removed from Santa-Land as it could possibly be. No children allowed here. Nothing wholesome about the place at all, with alcohol served without limit and a constant haze of cigarette smoke. Janie hated the way she smelled when she left the bar. She couldn't get home fast enough to shower and change.

She'd gotten the job at the Honcho a little over a month ago when she first moved into the area, but it wasn't working out. She needed a day job with regular hours.

Even though she wasn't anxious to go inside, Janie didn't dare linger in the parking lot. Not in this part of town.

Hurrying in, she stashed her purse under the bar and put on her apron, putting on a smile with it. No one knew or cared that the smile wasn't real.

She had accepted this job after a phone interview, believing the Honcho was a restaurant. Although they served a few Tex-Mex dishes, the Honcho was actually the neighborhood watering hole. The people who frequented the bar were there to either escape from or avoid going home. It wasn't what Janie had thought it to be at all, but with the rent coming due and other expenses, she stayed on.

"But I'm quitting as soon as I can," she murmured, encouraging herself as she made her way to a table with four men. Hopefully, being an elf at Filmore's would lead to a job as a salesclerk when the Christmas season was over. Until then, there wasn't much time for job hunting. She would stay at the Honcho until Christmas, then find something else.

Until Christmas. Her mind flashed to Santa, and she paused, distracted by the lights dancing from the mirror ball. Sparkling lights, reminding her of the twinkle of green eyes that crinkled at the corners, gorgeous eyes above a white angel-hair beard.

Then she remembered how she'd had to ask him to unzip her dress and the heat of embarrassment hit her cheeks. Shaking herself into action, she moved among her tables, willing herself to forget the whole zipper incident.

The four guys at the table whistled again, calling her over.

"Hey, baby! Over here."

Janie nodded at the man she'd labeled Jerk Number One and threaded her way through the crowded, smoke-filled room to get to his table.

"What'll it be, guys?" she asked, forcing a smile as she noticed the manager looking her way.

"Aw, you know what we like, baby," Jerk drawled. He'd had a few already and probably didn't need more, but the Happy Honcho didn't enforce a limit. As long as the customer was willing to pay, they were willing to pour.

"Longnecks all around, right?" she asked brightly.

"You got it, baby." Jerk put his arm around her waist, squeezing her to his side.

Janie forced a laugh and stepped away. "I'll get those drinks right to ya."

She hurried to the bar to place her order, oblivious of the man sitting in the corner of the room watching her every move.

The manager leaned against the bar, keeping an eye on his domain.

"Those guys at table six are coming on too strong," she told him. "They've had way too much to drink."

The manager took a long drag on his cigarette, exhaling the smoke in her face. "I don't care what they're doing. Do your job and keep their glasses filled."

Gritting her teeth, Janie took the tray of drinks to the table.

They made their big play, dropping their money on the floor and making a big show of "helping" her retrieve it, just so they could get their hands on her. She was so spitting mad and frustrated, she didn't know whether to screech or cry or both.

Out of nowhere, a man pushed between her and her tormentors.

Nick faced down the largest of the jerks, aching for the release of punching out this piece of scum. He'd sat in the corner watching Janie at work, a slow burn building every time a guy made a pass at her. It shouldn't have mattered to him, and maybe if he'd just once seen the same smile on her face as he did in Santa-Land he could've walked out of here. Let her live her double life. But the fear and desperation he saw in her face wouldn't let him go.

"Leave the lady alone," he growled.

The nearest jerk shrank back, intimidated by six-foot-four and over two hundred pounds of sheer hostility. Nick had seen that look before on the faces of linebackers he was up against in a big game. At those times, the competition was so intense he didn't see the opposition as people or friends, but as obstacles to be put out of the way.

But the other men didn't see Nick's glare and were too drunk to resist a challenge. One threw a punch he easily avoided. He glanced around, looking for a way out. His freedom depended on staying out of trouble and a barroom brawl would put him away. Anyway, the point wasn't to fight this creep but to keep Janie safe.

Turning to her, he took her arm and said, "Come on, Janie. Let's get out of here."

Surprisingly, she pulled away. Nick gaped as she glared at him.

"Leave me out of this," she said, shielding herself with her tray and stepping back.

The manager of the Honcho pushed his way toward them.

"What's the problem, Janie?" he asked.

"Nothing," she replied, smile back in place. "Just a misunderstanding among the guys."

"Yeah, right," the manager muttered, taking in the situation. "Okay, Judd, what's the deal?"

The jerk who threw the punch straightened with a smirk. "We were paying our bill and talking to Janie when this guy decided to butt in and start some trouble."

Nick waited for the manager to turn and recognize him, but it didn't happen. Instead, he turned on Janie.

"That's it, Janie. You're fired. Don't try waitressing anymore until you can learn how to get along with the customers—and that includes leaving your boyfriend at home."

"You can't do that. I don't even know this guy—"

"Get out of here and quit causing a scene. Or do you want one of the bouncers to escort you out?"

Janie took a deep breath and closed her eyes, visibly reeling her emotions under control. Without saying another word, she turned and carried her tray to the bar, the manager and Nick following her.

"Don't expect to collect any severance pay," her boss said, then turned and walked away.

Again, Nick took Janie's arm.

"Come on, Janie, let me take you home."

She went with him quietly enough, only stopping to collect her purse. Once they got outside the bar in the cool night air, she pulled away from him.

"Look, thanks for your help. I really appreciate your sticking up for me against those creeps. But I think you need to leave me alone now."

"Not until I make sure you get home safely," Nick

responded. When she shook her head, he asked, "Why not, Janie?"

"How do you know my name? I've never seen you here before." Hands on hips, she swept him with a glance from head to toe, then came back to his face. Her hands dropped from her hips and she took a step back. "Oh, my gosh. You're Nick Klaus from TV!"

Nick grinned. "Yeah, that's me. I just realized—"

"What are you doing here?"

The question shook Nick and he scuffed the broken sidewalk with his feet. He shouldn't be here at all. The terms of his probation were very clear. No bars. But something had urged him to follow Janie when she'd left Filmore's that evening. He'd had a foreboding that all was not well with the sweet-faced elf who'd walked out the door with a grim expression rather than the cheeriness he sensed was her natural demeanor.

"I just wanted to get to know you better." That statement would have sent most women into a frenzy, he knew. He'd seen the effect before. So he wasn't prepared for Janie's reaction.

She snorted. "I already know you well enough to tell you I'm not your type. Find someone else to hit on." With that she turned and stalked toward her car.

Nick started after her. "Me hit on you? Hey, I was the one who got those creeps to leave you alone."

She stopped walking. Nick could see her profile, lit by the streetlight as she tossed her words over her shoulder. "Yeah, and you cost me my job. But that's nothing to you, a big football commentator. You make millions of dollars. You have no idea what it's like to have to hold down two jobs just to put food on the table."

That hurt. It was true—except it was thousands not millions—but it hurt. "I'm sorry about you being fired. I didn't like watching those guys putting the moves on you."

Janie swung around, her purse swinging wide on its shoulder strap. Nick stepped back to keep from being hit with it. "What's it to you?" she demanded.

Again, Nick was stuck without an answer. Why had those guys gotten under his skin? Why had he bothered to follow Janie here at all?

"Look, I'm sorry," he said. "Let me buy you a cup of coffee—"

"I have to get home," she said, her tone cold enough to form icicles. "Good-bye." As she reached into her purse to get her keys, the strap slipped off her shoulder and the purse fell. The impact with the pavement scattered the contents in all directions. Janie scrambled to gather everything up and stuff it back in the purse. Nick tried to help but she didn't give him a chance. She was starting up her car while he still picked up things from the pavement.

"Wait," he called, but it was too late. Tires spitting loose gravel, Janie sped from the parking lot, leaving Nick holding her wallet.

Chapter Two

Janie's hands shook on the steering wheel as she guided her car through the late-night Dallas streets. *Oh, what a lovely day.* Everything that could go wrong had, right up to and including losing her job. That's what made her hands shake. It had nothing to do with the fact that Nick Klaus had come to her rescue. Nothing to do with his tousled hair, the dimple in his chin, or charismatic personality. No, Nick Klaus was nothing to her.

He was notorious. All the tabloids said so.

She ground her teeth. The nerve of him, interfering with her life. As if she was one of those flighty women who swooned just because a handsome guy from TV looked her way. Well, she wasn't swooning. She was mad, plain mad, because . . . because . . .

A red light made her pause. She took a deep breath and let it out with a huff at the realization that she wasn't mad.

She was scared.

She could still see the concern in his eyes, the righteous light in them as he stood up to the drunks at the bar. She felt his touch on her arm as he guided her out of the bar. He affected her so much, it scared her.

Everyone knew Nick Klaus was bad news. Talented, spoiled, rich, he did everything to excess. His wrongdoings were constantly reported in the newspapers with the wink-and-a-nod, boys-will-be-boys attitude that said anything a sports hero did could be forgiven. There were many who only remembered Nick's fantastic plays, the number of quarterbacks he'd sacked, the fumbles he'd caused and recovered.

How dare this man, this jerk among jerks, how dare he speak to her? After what he did, getting her fired.

His acting like he knew her didn't make sense.

Her response to him didn't make sense. She recognized him, as if she knew him.

Well, who wouldn't? As famous as he was, or maybe infamous was the better word, on TV every night reporting the latest exploits on the gridiron.

But it wasn't as simple as that. Not just knowing his face from TV, but a feeling of familiarity, as if he were an old friend.

But he wasn't. No friend of hers. And she didn't want him to be a friend. No. He was bad news.

Another red light. Another pause that did nothing to slow her racing heart, the breaths that were almost sobs.

It wasn't the right place for you to work.

The thought brought her up short.

"But I need the job," she said aloud, arguing with her conscience.

Not that job. Nick isn't the problem. He was a blessing in disguise.

"Oh, he's in disguise all right," Janie muttered. "A wolf in sheep's clothing. I can't imagine why he decided to notice me at the Honcho."

The question echoed in her head as she parked outside her Greenville Avenue apartment.

Still fuming, she took the steps two at a time, then fitted her key in the lock and pushed open the door.

"Mommy!" A four-year-old tyke danced with delight at the sight of her mother. "You got home early!"

Janie swept her daughter in a hug. "That's right, pumpkin, but it's way past your bedtime." She glanced around the darkened apartment. "Where's Aunt Gloria?" she asked, referring to her roommate and best friend.

"She's asleep," the little girl whispered. "I needed a drink and I got one by myself." Her visible pride in her accomplishment enchanted Janie all over again with her little angel—her gleaming curls, round face, and big brown eyes.

Gloria, her blond hair flying as she bolted out of the room Carrie shared with Janie, stopped short when she saw the mother and child together. "Oh, there you are, Carrie. What are you doing up?"

"I was firsty."

"She got her own drink of water," Janie said, picking up the little girl and carrying her to the kitchen. "Did Carrie give you a hard time tonight?"

Gloria dismissed the question with a wave and followed them to the kitchen. "No problem. I fell asleep after the tenth time reading *The Three Bears*. I thought Carrie was asleep too."

"Do you need another drink?" Janie asked Carrie.

She shook her head, curls bouncing. "I'm full."

"Then it's time to get on to bed. I'll come tuck you in."

Janie followed Carrie as she scooted down the short entry hall into the bedroom and climbed into her trundle bed. She pulled the quilt up to Carrie's chin and kissed her forehead. "Good night, sweetie," she said.

"Say good night to BeBe." Carrie held up a stuffed bunny with long ears.

"Good night, BeBe," she said, stroking a long ear, the material soft from constant handling. How many times had she sewed those ears back on? BeBe was Carrie's lovey. The little girl wouldn't go to sleep without her.

Janie closed the door behind her and walked down the short hallway to the living room. Gloria puttered in the kitchen, making tea.

"You're home early," she repeated when Janie perched

on one of the high stools at the bar that separated the kitchen from the living room.

Janie sighed. "Yes, I'm early." Resting her chin on her hands, she watched her friend move about the kitchen. What was she going to do now? Without the job at the Honcho, she didn't see how she could meet her expenses. Glo was a great friend, always ready to help out with Carrie, but there had to be a limit to her generosity. In fact, Janie would insist on limits. She refused to take charity, even from her best friend.

Gloria set cups, tea bags, and sugar on the counter in front of Janie. She said, "Carrie's sweet. She really misses you on the nights you work at the Honcho. I wish you could find a better job."

"I'll be looking for a new one tomorrow." Choosing a teabag from the assortment in the box gave Janie an excuse to avoid her friend's eyes.

"Why, what happened?"

Janie shook her head. "You wouldn't believe it. *I* don't believe it."

Gloria regarded Janie as she stirred her tea. "Are you going to tell me or make me guess?"

"I'll tell. You'd never guess. Nick Klaus came into the Honcho tonight."

Gloria leaned forward, her tea forgotten. "Nick Klaus from TV? At the Honcho? Is he as good-looking in person? Were you his waitress? Tell me!"

Janie grimaced at her friend. "He's bad news and you

know it. Everyone knows it. It's a wonder he's allowed out on the streets after what he did."

Gloria waved that away. "What was he doing at the Honcho?"

Janie looked away. After condemning the man, she knew her next words would sound hypocritical. "He stood up for me when some drunks started hitting on me. The manager decided I had started the problem and fired me."

"Nick Klaus was your knight in shining armor." Gloria breathed the words with her hands clasped over her heart. "Oh, that's just too romantic. What did he do when the manager fired you?"

"He offered to buy me a cup of coffee."

Gloria squealed and bounced over to Janie. "And you got home early? Why aren't you still out with Nick?"

Janie picked up her teacup and sipped from it, trying to put some distance between herself and Gloria's enthusiasm. "Because I didn't go out with him, that's why. It wasn't romantic, Glo, it was weird. He knew my name. He spoke like he knows me. And I've never seen him in person before."

Looking off into the distance, Gloria said, "It's fate. He looked across that smoke-filled room and fell in love with you at first sight. He asked the other waitress for your name, and when he saw you needed help, he came to your rescue."

The temptation to believe in her friend's fairy tale was strong, but Janie held on to a practical streak. "He got me fired. All I have now is the job at Filmore's, and that won't last much longer."

Sniffing at the bursting of her bubble, Gloria turned back to her tea. "You at least gave him your phone number, didn't you?"

"No. You know I'm not interested in going out with anyone. I'm certainly not going to go out with someone like him."

"Maybe he's changed." At Janie's exasperated glare, Gloria recanted. "All right. It's just, I've had a crush on Nick Klaus for years. I know he's wild and bad."

"But you would've gone out with him."

"Yes. At least for a cup of coffee. But it's not just Nick, Janie. You won't go out with anybody."

Janie glanced toward the bedroom where Carrie lay sleeping. "Let's just say I was stupid in love once. I'm not going to make the same mistake again. I deserve better, and so does Carrie."

Gloria came around the bar and gave her friend a hug. "You deserve the best. Your knight in shining armor will come along some day, Janie. I hope you recognize him when he does."

Nick stretched out in the large chair behind the desk in his study. His house had been designed by a well-recommended architect and had all kinds of exclusive features, but Nick never felt at home in it. Like this room, the study. He had nothing to study. But it had seemed right, tonight, to bring Janie's wallet in here and set it on the desk in front of him. He had no couth; he had gone through it thoroughly, learning more about the elf who worked with him.

One bank card.

Cash, but not a lot.

Her driver's license.

A grocery list. Now, this was interesting. It listed what Nick considered usual stuff . . . bread, milk . . . but also some things he considered unusual for a—he checked the license—twenty-five-year-old girl. Who ate animal crackers anymore? Or applesauce? *Yechh.*

And what was this? A picture. A picture of an adorable little girl. Now, there was an angel. A little bitty girl with curly hair, round brown eyes, and a winsome smile stood on a chair. Nick had no idea how to judge the age of children but he knew she wasn't very old. Three or four, maybe. No bigger than a minute. She made Nick smile just looking at her.

That explained the animal crackers and applesauce.

It could also explain why Janie kept him at arm's length. Maybe she had a jealous husband to go along with that beautiful little girl.

But if he were that jealous, why would he let her work in a place like the Honcho?

Then there was the wallet itself. Dark blue, Velcro fastener. And Tigger, bouncing across the cover.

Tigger.

Nick knew women accused men of being stuck in childhood. It was a breakup line he'd heard several times. But the evidence, slim as it was, suggested Janie had childlike tendencies.

Which was kind of cute.

But then, he found everything about Janie cute. The way she walked. The way her curly hair bounced when she moved. That short tunic she wore at work. The way her eyes flashed when she confronted him after he'd gotten her fired from her job.

Ouch.

That had been a bad move. Not only did following her to the bar violate his probation, it'd gotten him off on a bad foot with her.

He'd just been trying to help. No woman deserved to be hustled like that.

Nick shrugged uncomfortably at the thought, remembering nights out with his friends when they acted the same way as those guys at the Happy Honcho. As he watched them make their moves, it had been like looking in a mirror at the not-too-distant past.

He hadn't liked what he saw. When he stood up to those guys, it wasn't just to protect Janie. He was trying to prove to himself he wasn't in the same league as they were, that he was better than them.

Only Janie hadn't appreciated his help.

He owed her. An apology and a job.

Tomorrow, come hail or high water, he'd deliver both to her. In person.

The phone rang at 7:30 AM. It was Nick's agent, announcing hail and high water.

"They fired you," Stan Wingate said. "They tried to dress it up, saying they haven't been satisfied with the ratings for a while and your name doesn't have the recognition it once did."

Nick couldn't think of a response. He understood why the TV execs fired him. Having a high-profile anchor involved in a felony case wasn't good publicity. It didn't fit the image the TV station wanted to project.

"It's a good thing my uncle gave me a job at Filmore's. The court says I have to be gainfully employed to meet the terms of my probation."

"It's beneath you, man." Stan had bigger plans in mind. "I'll put some feelers out, see what's out there. You could coach. Or act. That experience in front of the camera should come in handy."

Nick's body sagged against the chair. None of those things sounded good. But the Santa gig, by definition, wouldn't last forever. "Look, forget about that for now. Let's not even think about it until after Christmas."

"Can't promise that. After all, I don't get paid unless you get paid. It's my job to make sure Nick Klaus stays in the limelight."

"Yeah, I get it." Nick blew out a breath, leaned back in his chair, and stared at the ceiling. Fired. Just like Janie.

Now, there was an idea.

"Look, Stan, while you're putting out feelers, could you do me a favor?"

"What kind of favor?" Stan sounded wary. Nick wondered if his agent was considering dropping him, if this phone call was a preliminary skirmish. Next he'd hear how nothing was out there. Finally, Stan would have to let him go. The scenario gave Nick a sour taste.

"Nothing. Never mind. Call me if you turn up something." Nick hung up.

The favor he wanted to ask was help in finding a job for Janie. In fact, he'd meant to call the TV studio and see if they had anything available for her. The only reason he hadn't was he didn't know enough about her to recommend her for a job.

She had waitressing skills. She was good with children.

He reached for the wallet on his desk, smiling at the picture of Tigger. The Velcro fastener made a ripping sound as he opened it. He pulled out Janie's driver's license and the picture behind it. Setting the picture beside the license, he compared Janie's image to the little girl's. The eyes and noses had the same set to them. Mother and daughter.

What did that tell him?

He'd heard that kids were expensive—clothes, daycare, and doctors all cost money. Being a bachelor, he'd always ducked out whenever talk turned to kids. He and his siblings had been raised by nannies, hardly ever being around their parents until they were deemed grown up enough to appear with them in public. That was part of the reason he loved football: the camaraderie of the team, the guidance of the coaches. In football, he had found a family. A family he missed more each day since having to leave it.

So, Janie had a child to support. Nothing in the wallet indicated a man in her life. That explained why she was working two jobs.

And he'd lost her the one that paid the best.

He would make it up to her. Her address was on her license. He'd go over there, give her back her wallet, and talk about what kind of job she might like to have.

And maybe she could help him find one for himself.

Janie sat at the kitchen table, a sketchbook in front of her. She enjoyed designing her own greeting cards for Christmas and decided to work out some ideas this morning before the workday started. In a minute, Carrie would be up. She needed to clear up her papers but put it off in favor of lingering over a picture of Santa. Adding a few lines around his eyes, she smiled at the way they crinkled with just the right blend of amusement. She found herself wondering what he looked like under the whiskers, then pushed away the paper and pencil when she realized she'd sketched the young Santa she worked with at Filmore's.

"What'cha doing, Mommy?" Carrie wandered into

the kitchen in her PJs, clutching BeBe and sucking on her finger.

"I've been drawing. Did you have a good sleep?" Janie eyed the long-suffering bunny, wondering when she would be able to sneak it away to the washer. Maybe if she let Carrie take a bath with it . . .

"Uh, huh." Carrie climbed onto the chair across from Janie. The doorbell rang. "I'll get it!" Carrie tried to climb down too fast and slipped, bumping her head on the table.

Janie scooped her up and headed toward the door, kissing the boo-boo as she walked.

The blood soared to her cheeks when she opened the door and recognized the man standing there, in spite of his dark glasses and the cap pulled low over his face.

Nick Klaus.

He spoke. She watched his lips move but didn't hear a word he said. Alarm bells, buzzers, sirens rang in her mind with the refrain, *What is he doing here?*

Carrie squirmed, and Janie turned from Nick's magnetic presence to set the child down and watch her scamper back toward the kitchen. The break gave her a chance to regain her equilibrium. Straightening, she demanded, "What do you want?"

Nick took a deep breath and snatched off his cap, looking like an overgrown schoolboy caught in a scrape. "Janie, I apologize for getting you fired last night. If you want, I'll call the manager and explain what happened. Or I can help you find another job."

For a moment, he looked so appealing, so sweet, she was tempted to let him come in. But he kept talking.

"I know a lot of people down at the TV station. I'm sure we could find a job there for you. Whatever you want. Just tell me and I'll look into it."

The flash of friendliness she'd started to feel vanished, replaced by a surge of hurt pride.

He was making her his charity case.

She didn't need his handouts. She opened her mouth to tell him so—

"Mommy!"

The cry sent Janie racing through the apartment to the kitchen, Nick on her heels.

An overturned gallon jug of milk glugged its contents over the table and on to the floor. Carrie stood on a chair, regarding them with wide eyes while she sucked her index finger.

"Oh, Carrie. What happened?" Janie righted the milk jug as she spoke and grabbed the paper towels. She pulled at the end, the towels billowing in an arc as they came off the roll and settled in the milk on the floor. Tearing those towels off, she pulled out another ream and settled that one on the table.

A large, lone tear tracked down Carrie's cheek. "I was firsty. I tried to get some more milk but it was too big."

Nick had a flashback to his own childhood and some mess he had made trying to be a big boy and do something by himself. And the scolding and punishment he had gotten. To his surprise, Janie didn't scold.

"You mean you lifted the milk jug to the table by your-self? My goodness, that takes a lot of strength. Here, use the paper towels to wipe up the milk."

Carrie pushed at the milk with the paper towel, send-ing a wavelet across the table toward some papers. As Nick grabbed for them, his hand hit a glass of milk. It arced off the table, on to the floor, splattering Janie with its contents.

Her glare should've fried him on the spot.

When she saw what he held, she left off sopping up milk and hurried to his side.

"Are those all right?" she asked, gesturing to the ob-jects he held.

Nick looked at the papers . . . and was spellbound. The papers were actually sketches. A portrait of him, in his Santa suit. A scene at Filmore's, of the children lined up to meet Santa, with impatient mothers checking their watches. A Christmas angel, looking very much like the little girl standing on the chair at the table.

"These are great," he said, handing them to her with reverence.

She flashed him a look that at first seemed pleased, then changed to annoyance as a drop of milk dripped from her hair on to the paper.

"I'll just put these away," she mumbled, pushing past him to the bedroom door.

That left Nick and Carrie staring at each other.

Carrie took her finger out of her mouth long enough to ask, "What's your name?"

"I'm Nick Klaus." Nick gave her his best smile and nod. "I work with your mom at Filmore's."

Her eyes grew rounder than ever. "Mommy works with Santa Claus," she whispered in an awestruck voice. Then, after giving Nick a moment's consideration, "You don't look like Santa Claus."

How was he supposed to respond to that?

He rubbed the back of his neck, hoping that would push an idea into his brain. "Well, you know how famous people have to wear disguises sometimes?"

Carrie nodded. "Are you in gus-dize?"

"That's right." It was even the truth, to a point. "But I'll be back to normal at Filmore's. Are you going to come visit me?"

"Oh, yes!"

Janie entered the room with a towel around her head. Lifting Carrie down from the chair, she said, "I set out your clothes, sweetie. Scoot on in and get dressed. It's a daycare day."

"All right." Turning to Nick, Carrie surprised him by giving him a big wink—or what for her was a big wink, with her nose and eyes all scrinched up. " 'Bye, Mr. Claus."

Nick's heart went *ping!* as he fell completely and totally in love with the little girl. " 'Bye, Carrie," he choked out past a sudden lump in his throat.

Once they were alone, Nick took a deep breath and took up where he left off.

"Janie, I feel responsible for getting you fired last

night, but I'm sure I can help you find another job. Just give me a copy of your resumé—"

Janie looked up from wiping the milk and gave a brief, unamused laugh. "My resumé." She stood, shaking her head and turned on him with full-force hostility. "I don't know why you're here, or how you found out where I worked and where I live. As for what happened last night, if that's the way you help people then you'd better stay away from me. I am not your charity case." Tossing the towel onto the table, she walked to the front door and held it open. "Get out."

Nick had been tackled by three-hundred-pound guys with less punch than this pronouncement.

"I came here to help you."

"I don't need your help. Good-bye."

He stepped out, remembered the wallet, and turned, only to have the door shut firmly in his face.

Chapter Three

An hour later, stripped to his underwear in the restroom at Filmore's, he began the transformation from Nick Klaus to Santa Claus.

The suit first: pants, tunic, belt, boots. Thick and bulky, the red velvet suit hid the athletic body beneath.

Next came the face makeup. The older Santa, Mr. Hopkins, being endowed with natural white hair, didn't use makeup or the angel-hair beard. He'd been Filmore's official Santa for years and wasn't pleased with the young interloper, but poor health had forced him to cut back his hours. Whatever the reason, Nick was glad to disguise his too-well-known face any way he could. Maybe it was cowardly, hiding this way, but until the hue and cry over the accident died down, he felt it was best for all concerned for Nick Klaus to disappear.

As he worked, his familiar features did seem to disappear. The beard covered the lower half of his face, hiding his wide mouth and square chin. A long white wig covered his brush of ginger hair. Eyebrow makeup—amazing, what a big business Santa Claus was; he even had eyebrow makeup—completed the effect. All that white made his eyes appear green rather than the blue listed on his driver's license. It all depended on what color he wore. Cap on, and the look was complete.

Nick Klaus looked in the mirror. Santa Claus looked back.

If only he could change his life as easily as he changed his appearance. He needed to do more than just mask and cover up. He needed to change from the inside out. If he just had a clue how to do it.

Nick's body ached as he adjusted his belt. The pain and stiffness were the legacy of seven years of using his body as a battering ram in the NFL. And three years before that in college. And high school before that.

He'd used drugs and alcohol to numb the physical pain, welcoming the fact it also dulled the emotional pain of having nothing in his life besides football. All of his life was playing football. It was the only thing he was good at.

He would never have given it up, except he had no choice. Someone's shoulder had been harder than his knee, leaving it crushed to bits. No way he could get back on a football field. He added prescription painkillers to his list of feel-good remedies.

The TV gig had been fun and allowed him to hang with his friends from the NFL, but he didn't really belong with them. His life and their lives weren't the same. The longer he was out of football, the less he belonged anywhere. Each passing season put distance between him and what had made him famous. He wasn't that good a broadcaster, and the cachet of having Nick Klaus announce was stale. It had been getting that way even before the accident.

The TV suits were right. His exploits on the football field were over and done with. He couldn't live on that fading glory for the rest of his life.

It wasn't that he hadn't tried to re-invent himself over the years. With the changes in his career, he'd promised himself to do better, to clean up his act. His resolution lasted until the next party—and there'd always been a party. The only surprising thing about the wreck was it hadn't happened sooner. Or been more deadly. Everyone told him how lucky he was to walk away from it and especially fortunate that the girl with him had survived and would make a full recovery. Maybe the real blessing was that he had to leave his wild ways behind. Get clean and sober. Get a life.

He didn't need money. When he was a player, he'd let his father convince him to have his paycheck sent to an investment firm. It meant living on an allowance but they'd made his money work for him. Finances were no problem. The problem was, he was unskilled labor who had to be gainfully employed for the next three years.

So, here he was, a has-been at thirty. No talent. No degree, since he had quit college to go to the pros. Nothing but a temporary job playing Santa.

"Ho ho ho," he told his reflection, his mood anything but jolly. He left the restroom and headed through the breakroom to the store. On his way, he saw Janie pushing her street clothes into her locker.

May as well get it over with, he thought, pulling her wallet out of his pocket. At least there was no one around to hear if she told him off again like she had earlier. Hopefully, he could persuade her to keep his identity secret.

"Hi, Janie."

She glanced up, gave a brief smile, and closed and locked her locker before responding. "Hi, Santa."

Santa? True, he was in costume but—

"Thanks for helping me out last night. You know, with my zipper."

"Sure. My pleasure. I mean"—he proffered her wallet—"I picked this up in the parking lot last night—"

"Oh, my! I didn't even know I'd dropped it. I was in such a hurry leaving here last night . . . I never zip my purse . . . thanks." She took the wallet from him, then turned back to her locker and began spinning the combination lock. After stuffing the wallet in her purse and zipping it closed, she slammed the locker door and smiled at him. "Thanks, again. That was really kind of you."

They stood a moment, smiling at each other, both

tongue-tied, until Janie said, "I guess it's time to get started."

"Yeah." He'd never been so flummoxed in his life. She appeared to have no idea Nick Klaus and Filmore's Santa were one and the same.

Not bad. He wouldn't tell, and no one else knew. In better spirits, Nick offered Janie his arm. She hesitated a second, then slipped her hand in the crook of his elbow. They walked side by side down the aisles of the store to Santa-Land. Nick took his seat and waited for Janie to bring over the first victim, um, sweet child. He picked up the little boy, set him on his knee, and asked, "What do you want for Christmas?"

The morning passed with a quickness that surprised Janie. She felt good, cheerful, like the weight of the world had been lifted off her shoulders. Apparently, she had been more stressed about her job at the bar than she realized. Nick Klaus had actually done her a favor by getting her fired.

The thought of Nick and how kind he'd been left her feeling uncomfortable. She'd been ungracious when he tried to help. But meeting him face to face and being hit full impact with his charisma had both excited and alarmed her. Excited, because she had as big a crush on him as every other woman in the Dallas/Fort Worth area. Alarmed, because of the resemblance he had to her ex-husband, Carrie's father.

True, that relationship had been an eternity ago—

starting their first year of college. They'd insisted on getting married against the wishes of both families. When their parents had cut off financing for college, they'd agreed she would work while he went to school, then he would do the same for her when he completed his degree. Unfortunately, while she worked, he not only went to classes, he also hung out with his friends and played on intramural teams. He lived the complete college experience that Janie worked and paid for.

Carrie's unexpected arrival on the scene changed everything . . . for the worse. He chafed at the responsibilities of having a young family. As soon as he graduated, he found a job in another state and left without a backward glance.

Ancient history. For the present, she had a beautiful little girl and a string of low-paying jobs on her resumé. She might not have a college degree, but her ex-husband had taught her not to trust her own judgment when it came to men.

So, no matter how kind Nick Klaus had been, her first reaction was to put up walls to keep him out. She was *not* going to be used and hurt ever again.

She printed out a picture of twin girls, each one sitting on one of Santa's knees, and placed it in a cardboard frame. "Thank you," she told the proud parents before turning to look for the next child in line.

No one there. They'd worked without a break since starting. This was the first breather they'd had.

Santa stood and stretched. "Is it time to feed the reindeer?"

She couldn't help smiling at the euphemism, taken from the sign they had to post whenever Santa left Santa-Land. "Sure. You go on. I'll put up the sign."

It took just a second to put the sign up, and Santa waited for her. Together, they walked back to the break-room.

The room had been outfitted with a table and chairs in the center. Drink and snack machines stood at attention along one wall. A refrigerator was in the corner next to a long counter holding a microwave and a sink. A sofa that was rumored to be a reject from the furniture department sat sagging along the wall opposite the vending machines. People came and went, stopping and gossiping for a few minutes before heading back into the store.

Most of the salesclerks ignored the seasonal work-ers, so Janie tried to stay out of their way. She carried her cup of yogurt to the sofa instead of the table, where several clerks sat and talked together. To her surprise, Santa joined her on the couch, bringing along a nutri-tion supplement drink that he sipped from a straw.

"Have you ever heard so much gossip?" he asked Janie, shaking his head. "If you sneezed in housewares, they'd know about it in the bargain basement in three seconds flat."

Janie nodded her agreement. Santa had turned out differently than she'd thought. From his teasing, she'd figured him for an incorrigible flirt. She dealt with that kind of guy by giving him the cold shoulder. But she couldn't look right through someone who'd gone out of his way to help her. She'd be nice. After all, they had to work together for the next few weeks.

When she finished her yogurt, she tossed the cup into the trash, then washed her spoon at the sink. As she dried the spoon and her hands with a paper towel, she noticed the usual babble had died into silence. Glancing around, she saw she and Santa were alone in the room.

Just like last night. She looked at him, a shiver of memory passing along her spine as she remembered him unzipping her dress. Noticing her scrutiny, he raised his eyebrows at her in question.

"Thanks again for helping me last night," she blurted. "And for returning my wallet this morning."

Santa pulled the straw away from his lips, careful not to get any drops on the pristine white of his beard. "No problem," he said.

For a moment, neither said anything, just looked at each other, green eyes into brown.

Janie blinked first. Clearing her throat, she said the first thing that came into her head. "You could take that costume off when you're eating. Then you wouldn't have to worry about getting food in your beard."

The beard around Santa's mouth moved, and Janie guessed he grinned at her.

"What costume?"

The guy could not be serious! She smiled, in spite of herself. "When you're not playing Santa."

"Who's playing?"

She laughed outright. "Next thing, you'll be telling me your name is Nicholas."

"Actually, it's Nicodemus."

"Really?" His joking and her curiosity penetrated her resolve to stay distantly polite. Intrigued, she pulled out a chair and sat at the table.

"Yep." He nodded. "Is your name really Janie?"

"Yes, it is."

He wagged a warning finger at her. "You shouldn't lie to Santa."

Heat surged up her neck and into her cheeks. "How did you know? Oh! You saw my driver's license."

"I looked in the wallet to see who it belonged to. Janae isn't such a bad name."

"No, but it's unusual. People misspell it all the time. It's easier to say Janie and let them spell it that way."

"It's better than my sister's name." His eyes crinkled with humor. "For some reason, my parents named her D'Monique. My brother and I always called her Domino. She hated that."

"I'd hate it too."

"My brother's name is Quinn," Santa went on. "It doesn't sound bad, until you realize he's Quinn because he's the fifth. I had to sign an oath in blood saying I would never reveal his real name."

Janie laughed. "Why were you the lucky one, to be called Nicodemus?"

"It's an old family name on my mother's side. Every generation has one guy named Nicodemus. I'm it for this generation."

The normality of the conversation reassured Janie. Santa wasn't hitting on her, they were just talking. "When Carrie, my daughter, was born, I promised myself that I wouldn't inflict a strange name on her. Her name is pretty plain, but at least people don't mispronounce it."

"Didn't your husband have any say in naming her?"

Heat stung her neck and cheeks. So much for having a normal conversation. She'd walked right into that one. "My *ex*–husband didn't really care at that point what I did."

"Your daughter's cute. I saw her picture in your wallet."

Relief cooled her cheeks. "She's a doll. Of course, as her mother, I think she's wonderful."

Santa grinned. Janie stared at his lips, barely visible in the mass of angel hair. Her eyes came up to meet his, those dynamite green eyes, crinkling at the corners. His grin grew wider.

Heat returning to her cheeks, Janie stood. "We'd better get back to Santa-Land."

Not waiting for a response, she rushed out the door, hurrying so he couldn't catch up to her. She needed a minute alone, to get control of herself. It wasn't like her to open up like that to a man. Just because he'd found her wallet didn't mean he was trustworthy.

Except he'd given it back to her. And hadn't made fun of her name. He hadn't even blinked when she admitted she was a single mother. Which all added up to . . .

Nothing. Like she wanted it.

Even as the thoughts went through her mind, her fingertips tingled as if remembering his touch. The skin along her spine seemed extra sensitive, recalling how he'd unzipped her tunic.

Stopping at the gate to Santa-Land, she took a deep breath, trying to wipe away the errant sensations. The last thing she needed in her life was to develop a crush on Santa Claus.

Nick sat alone in the breakroom, giving Janie time to make her getaway.

Amazing.

Even after talking with him, Janie didn't connect Santa with Nick Klaus.

True, in the Santa getup there was no way anyone could tell what he actually looked like. Last night, Janie hadn't let him explain about how he knew her. Even today, she didn't let him explain about finding her wallet, just jumped to the nearest conclusion.

On the other hand, she'd finally thawed a bit to his teasing. Santa's teasing.

She didn't like Nick Klaus. Wouldn't even accept a

cup of coffee from him after he'd protected her from being hit on by a bunch of drunken guys.

What did all this tell him?

"Women are crazy," he muttered as he walked back to Santa–Land.

A line waited. When he came into view, some of the kids jumped up and down, waving to him in excitement. Others peeked at him from behind their mothers. When he came up next to them at the entrance, a red-haired boy at the head of the line leaned back, looking up, up, up at him. Nick looked down at the boy and tried to smile reassuringly.

"Hi," he said.

The kid cringed behind his mom.

Nick took his seat and beckoned to the boy. "C'mon over, champ."

The little guy shook his head and hid behind his mother.

"I'm sorry," the woman said. "I don't know what's wrong. He's been looking forward to seeing Santa."

"It's all right," Janie said. She addressed the child. "Why don't you watch how we take the pictures? When you're ready for your turn, just let me know. My name's"—she shot a sideways smile at Santa—"Elf Janie. Okay?"

Everyone nodded and the boy and his mom moved to the side.

Next up, a pink-wrapped bundle. A baby. Janie took

the infant from her mother and handed her to Nick. Prickles of panic went up his back.

"Isn't there a height or age requirement, Elf Janie?" Nick asked, sweat breaking out on the back of his neck. He'd never, ever, touched a baby.

"Just put your arm out like this, so she can rest on it, and hold her like this with your other hand. There. Sit still while I get back to the camera."

Nick held the baby as instructed and looked into her big brown, solemn eyes. She knew she was in the hands of a rookie. The corners of her little mouth turned down, making a perfect upside-down U before she scrunched her face up tight—

"Janie!" Santa looked up in desperation just as the camera flashed and the baby let out a wail.

"It's all right, it's all right, little one." Janie came to the rescue, picking up the infant and cuddling her. She grinned down at Santa. "All right?"

"Yeah. Maybe I should take the picture and you should sit here." The baby had quit crying and cooed at Janie.

Women! They were in cahoots, trying to make him look bad. But it was the most playful he'd seen Janie. He admired her tenderness with the kids.

"Okay, let's try something different." Janie carried the baby to the camera and made some adjustment, causing a light to flash in the front. She came back to Nick. "Okay, hold your arms like I showed you and look at the camera, no matter what." Keeping an eye on the flashing light, she counted down, ". . . five, four, three, two . . ." She plunked the baby into his arms and stepped out of the way just before the flash went off.

Startled, both Nick and the baby sat while Janie checked on the picture. "Perfect. Wait until you see this."

"I want to see the first picture," the baby's mother said, as she saved Nick by taking the child from his arms. "The expression on Santa's face was priceless."

Janie printed out that picture too. The women stood and giggled together, then showed Nick. Yep. He looked like a complete fool in the first picture. The second turned out very well—he almost looked like he knew what he was doing, holding a baby.

Then they added insult to injury by showing the pictures to everyone in line.

"I'll buy both pictures," the woman said. "They'll be so cute in her first Christmas album. Thank you, Elf Janie. Thank you, Santa."

Nick felt a nudge against his knee. The shy little guy leaned against him, a smile on his freckled face.

"My turn!" he said. "I want my picture just like the baby's."

"Just like the baby's?" Nick repeated.

"You mean, you want to race the camera the way we did with the baby?" Janie asked.

The boy nodded his head.

Janie looked at Santa and winked. "All right. Let me set the camera." She made the adjustment, the light started blinking. "Ready, Santa?"

"Ready!" Nick braced himself.

". . . Five, four, three . . ." Janie picked up the kid under his arms and heaved him into Nick's lap.

"Two . . ."

Nick had a second to get the boy pointed in the right direction.

"One!"

The picture was one of the best, capturing the excitement on the boy's face and a real smile from Nick.

And so it went, the rest of the afternoon. An atmosphere of fun encompassed Santa-Land. Santa and Elf Janie became a team, joking and laughing with each other and the children.

At the end of the day, they walked together to the back. Janie turned toward her locker, and Nick headed into the breakroom. He looked at the vending machines, digging into his pocket for change. Nothing there. He checked his right pocket. *Nada.* Frustrating. He had plenty of money in his wallet but he kept that in his locker. No way would he let some accident betray his disguise.

"My treat, tonight," Janie said, from behind him.

He turned. She was still in costume with her street clothes over her arm and her purse slung over her shoulder. It gaped open, unzipped, and she had her wallet in her hand. Taking out a couple of bills, she put the money into the machine. "As a thank-you," she explained. "For helping me last night and finding my wallet. Go ahead, pick what you want."

"Only if you'll join me," Nick told her.

She hesitated a fraction of a second, then nodded, her cheeks turning pink.

Nick pressed the button and pulled the bottle from the machine, then stepped back to let her buy a drink for herself. They carried their sodas to the sofa and sat together.

"You're not in a hurry tonight," he said.

She shook her head. "Nope. I don't have to hurry like that anymore." She sipped her drink, avoiding his eyes, as if stricken by shyness.

Nick tried to get the conversation ball rolling. "You took some great pictures today. You've got a good eye. And fast reflexes."

"You've got some good reflexes yourself. You managed to catch those kids pretty well."

"That's what it's all about—making the kids happy."

She nodded. "You're right. The kids are what's important at Christmas. Or any other time." She glanced at her watch. "Speaking of kids, I need to get home to Carrie." Standing, she gathered her things together. "I had fun today."

"Me too." Nick started to stand but she waved him back to his seat.

"You don't have to get up. I have to go change." She went into the restroom. When she emerged a few minutes later, she wore jeans and a sweater. Hanging the elf costume on a hook outside the restroom, she turned to go.

"See you tomorrow, Elf Janie."

She paused, looked directly into his face, and smiled. "See you tomorrow, Santa."

Chapter Four

"**O**n the fourth day of Christmas, my true love gave to me . . ."

Unable to remember the lyrics, Nick whistled the rest of the tune as he made his way to Santa-Land. It wasn't the fourth day of Christmas, anyway, but the fourth day of December.

Twenty more days of disguise.

What would he do when he had to come out of hiding?

It wasn't just a disguise anymore but his only employment. What would he do after Christmas?

One day at a time, he reminded himself. Besides, laying low had the benefit of working with Janie.

But as he approached Santa-Land, he didn't see an elf. Instead, he was met by Big Mama Claus herself.

Big Mama was his nickname for the older, formidable

woman who was usually paired with Mr. Hopkins, the older Santa. Not that he'd ever call her that to her face. He wasn't that stupid.

No elf tunic for this lady. More of a grandma type, she wore the full Mrs. Santa costume: long red dress, white frilled apron, little red cap perched on her iron-gray hair. Half-glasses rested on the end of her nose, and she was forever giving him the evil eye over the rims.

She scared him.

Scared the kids too. Not that she did anything overtly mean but she didn't connect with them the way Janie did. No racing the camera. No jokes. Very businesslike. She'd greet the tykes at the gate and escort them to him. While he got them settled on his knee, she went to the camera and picked up a stuffed animal. The only thing he ever heard her say to the kids was, "Smile at the teddy bear." And, *click,* that was that.

Between the two of them in those red costumes, they scared a lot of little kids. It took a pretty elf like Janie to keep them calm.

Where was the elf? He didn't get a chance to ask until the first reindeer feeding.

"I thought Janie was working today," he commented to Big Mama on the way to the breakroom.

She shot him an amused glance and said, "We switched days off this week. She needed to stay home with her daughter."

A clerk from women's wear, close to Big Mama's age, fell in step with them. "I hope she doesn't have that nasty stomach virus that's going around. I missed my day off last week because two of the part-timers called in and someone had to cover the floor." She tossed her head, conveying the sense that she was the only one who could do the job.

Relief brought Nick's heart back into the right place. Janie wasn't avoiding him, she just needed to spend time with Carrie. Or maybe job hunting. The last thought left a bad taste in his mouth, reminding him of his sins. If he'd followed his probation, never followed her to the bar, never interfered . . .

Then Janie would still be working in a bad situation, he'd never have met Carrie, and he'd still be exiled here, in Santa–Land, trying not to panic the little ones who trusted the suit.

After the break, he climbed back onto his throne in Santa–Land, regarding the line of kids with concern. He felt sorry for them. Here they'd been told all their young lives not to talk to strangers and now their mamas told them to go up and sit in the lap of someone they'd never met before and who was dressed funny to boot. No wonder they cried.

Recalling the techniques of some of his favorite coaches and remembering how Janie approached the kids with her soft voice and calm manner, he tried a different routine. When Big Mama escorted a little girl to him, he bent over, held out his hand and softly said, "Howdy. I'm Santa. What's your name?"

"Chelsea." The name came out with a lisp, due to missing front teeth.

"Hey, Chelsea, I bet all you want for Christmas is your two front teeth." Nick drew the little girl, all ruffles and pigtails, closer and pointed toward the camera. "Show Mrs. Claus that beautiful grin."

Chelsea smiled in all her gap-toothed glory, and Big Mama snapped the picture.

Talking broke the ice better than ho ho ho. And it wasn't one-sided. After introductions and a comment on a pretty dress or cool shoes, the kids just opened up and told him their life story.

During their lunch break, Big Mama surprised him.

"Not bad, Santa," she said, a smile taking the sting out of that over-the-glasses perusal. "You're beginning to get the knack of working with children."

Nick shrugged, though his ears burned. "They sure like to talk."

"They like when someone listens to them." Pausing before pushing open the door, she gave him another smile. "And you really listen. It means the world to them."

Nick continued to really listen throughout the day. He heard more stories than he did Christmas lists. He got the inside scoop on family, school, homework, sleepovers—you name it, he heard about it.

Later on, in the breakroom after his shift, he sat on the sofa with his bum knee stretched out, wondering who had listened to him when he was a kid. Not his parents. They'd been too busy with careers and social climbing to pay attention except when he got in trouble. His older brother and sister had been his playmates until they outgrew childhood games and grew into the same social game-playing his parents did. As for himself, the only game he ever played was on the gridiron.

And the only people who listened to him now were members of his AA group.

Big Mama came into the breakroom, dressed for success in a navy pantsuit. Out of the red costume, she looked friendlier, more approachable.

"Are you still here?" she asked. "I've always heard those Santa costumes are uncomfortable. And I know that one is dirty from the children. That last one was a real drooler."

"Yeah. Her mother said her name was Julia but I think she meant Droolia." Nick dabbed at the sodden front of his tunic with a handkerchief. The store saw to it that the costumes were cleaned at the end of each day, and Nick had a spare tunic in case of accidents. Before this job, he'd thought accidents meant spilling coffee. Wrong!

"Well, I was thankful it wasn't dripping from her chin in the picture." She turned to go but Nick called out to her.

"Mrs. . . . I've forgotten your name."

She turned and smiled. "It's Doris. Doris Coleman. And yours?"

Whoa. Forbidden territory. But he needed to tell her something.

"Just call me Santa."

Doris laughed. "You must be an actor. Once in character, always in character."

Nick grinned. "Close. But, Mrs. Coleman, I was wondering if I could ask you a personal question."

Eyebrows raised, she responded, "You can ask. I don't promise to answer."

Nick nodded. "Fair enough. Is this your only job?"

Doris nodded.

"And does it pay enough for you to, say, rent an apartment and buy groceries?"

"Are you asking how much I make?" Sniffing, she raised her chin, giving him one of those prim looks over her glasses. "Discussing pay is against company policy. Besides, what I make is probably not comparable to your paycheck. I'm a retired widow, and this supplements my income from my retirement plan and from social security. I'm not here because I really need the job but because I enjoy being in the store at this time of year. I worked for Filmore's almost thirty years before I retired."

"Oh." Nick still didn't know what he needed to know—if this job brought in enough money for Janie and Carrie to live on. It didn't sound like it. Thinking of Janie looking through the want ads all day while he worked made him want to help her even more. After all, he was responsible for her losing her job. He needed to help her in any way he could.

As with everyone else today, once Mrs. Coleman started talking to him, she didn't stop. She sat down, a nostalgic gleam in her eyes. "I've watched the world change in the last thirty years. When I began working, the store was open from nine until five with Sundays off. I feel sorry for the young ones who have families who have to work until nine at night or later." She sighed. "Well, I guess there's no turning back the clock. Good night, Santa."

"G'night," Nick responded, lost in thought.

As the other employees came through the back rooms on their way home for the night, Nick sat and really listened.

The store clerks were tired from the long day. They smiled or nodded at Santa as they came through but treated him as part of the scenery. Nick caught several tidbits of information as they headed home.

"What I want to know is how can I get a good commission when there's no one shopping?"

Nick recognized one of the clerks from men's wear walking past. Another one answered, "I know someone who works at the Filmore's in the northside mall. Same position we have. More commission."

"Who needs this downtown store?" the first one asked. "No parking. Inconvenient for shoppers. We don't offer anything different from the malls."

Nick thought about the neighborhood, with its high-rise office buildings and ritzy hotels. It struck him for the first time that Filmore's was the only retail outlet in the area. There were a few pharmacies and delis, and some nice restaurants, but no other retail.

A gaggle from the cosmetics counters walked through, smelling yummy from the perfume and makeup they tried to sell.

"I wish we had a full-fledged salon here," one said. "A lady came in today who had a banquet tonight. We helped her with her makeup, but she really needed a shampoo and style."

"That would be wonderful," another chimed in. "Or a day spa."

"Filmore's day spa?" questioned a third. "Who would come to Filmore's for a day spa?"

Nick had no idea what a day spa was but it sounded like a nice idea. And how about a gym? Not like those little exercise rooms at the hotels, but a fully equipped, state-of-the-art gym, complete with trainers.

When the last employee left and no one was around to see the transformation of Santa Claus into Nick Klaus, Nick changed out of his Santa suit.

Apparently, Filmore's had some problems, he thought. But what could anybody do? Give up the store? Didn't having five stores in the Metroplex mean Filmore's competed with itself? Hey, no team could win if everyone worked against each other.

Shaking his head, Nick pulled his cap so it cast a shadow over most of his face. This listening deal was one thing but thinking was hard.

Carrie had woken up unusually fussy that morning, complaining of a stomachache. Janie called Filmore's and switched days off with Mrs. Coleman. That way, she wouldn't lose any pay.

It had been a peaceful day, with Carrie taking long naps in the morning and afternoon while Janie started painting Christmas cards to send to family and close friends. Each one was different, crafted with the recipient's tastes and preferences in mind. She worked from the sketches she made during free moments. Luckily, they hadn't been ruined when Nick Klaus came over.

Thinking about Nick troubled Janie. Part of her wanted to stand and stare at him, while another part wanted to head for the hills. She'd met him in person twice now, and both times had ended in a literal mess. First, her being fired because of his interference. The second time, well, spilled milk wasn't as catastrophic as being fired but inconvenient nevertheless.

The guy was bad news, anyway you looked at it. He had a reputation as big as Dallas, and an ego to go with it. Why he had singled her out was a mystery. She wasn't going to let some big-time jock get anywhere near her. Falling for that kind of guy once in a lifetime was enough. She'd done the right thing when she closed the door in his face.

Think about pleasant things, she told herself, regarding the blank sheet of paper in front of her. This card was for Gloria. Minutes later, a face emerged under her paintbrush. A familiar face, with green eyes that crinkled just so at the corners, a long red cap with a white pom-pom on the end, a mass of white whiskers.

Santa. Smiling at her work, Janie wondered what he'd thought when she hadn't come in to Filmore's that day. Did he miss her?

She missed him.

The realization stopped her brush between the palette and the paper.

She missed him.

How weird.

I guess it's what you get used to, she mused as she started clearing up her paint supplies. She'd seen him almost every day for the last week. They spent hours together. It was only natural she'd become accustomed to his company. That's all it was that made her think of him. That, and painting Christmas pictures.

He had unzipped my dress.

Even now, her cheeks heated with embarrassment.

He'd found her wallet and knew her real name. Not even Gloria knew her real name.

He'd told her stories about his family. He hadn't flinched when he found out she was a single mother.

Pausing in her cleanup, she thought back over each and every encounter with Santa. How sweet he was. His expressive eyes twinkling at her. And were there dimples under that angel–hair beard?

No. Stop. Don't be a fool.

Giving herself a mental shake, she rattled the paintbrush in the jar of water, washing away the image of Santa from her mind as the paint washed out of the brush. Santa was a guy, like any other. Men could not be trusted.

They would tell you exactly what you wanted to hear, then waltz off without a backward glance.

"Santa's a guy in a suit," she told herself, looking at the card bearing his portrait. "Don't forget that."

Carrie came into the room, yawning and rubbing her eyes with one hand, dragging BeBe by an ear with the other.

"Did you have a good nap?"

Nodding, Carrie crawled onto the sofa with Janie and settled in her lap. Janie felt her forehead.

"I don't think you have any fever. Would you like some supper?"

"I'm hungry," Carrie said.

Janie carried her into the kitchen and set her on a stool. While they made grilled cheese sandwiches, Gloria came home from work.

"Mmm, grilled cheese. My favorite," she said.

"*My* favorite," Carrie responded, joining in the game. No matter what was served, both claimed it as their favorite. The effect of the game was Carrie ended up eating a variety of foods she might not otherwise have tried.

"I have a wonderful idea for what we can do tonight," Gloria said as they sat at the table. "We can put up the Christmas tree." Her blue eyes gleamed as she winked at Carrie. "How about that?"

"Christmas tree!" Carrie clapped her hands.

"Do you have a tree?" Janie asked Gloria.

"My grandmother gave me her old artificial tree last year. She bought a new one at an after-Christmas sale.

So, we have a tree. But we don't have any decorations. I thought we could make some."

"I have some craft magazines," Janie said. "We can get some ideas for ornaments from those."

Gloria pushed her chin-length blond hair behind her ears. "Oh, I'm not artsy-craftsy like you are, Janie. I thought I'd string some popcorn."

"My favorite!" Carrie sang out.

"My favorite," Gloria said. "But not to eat this time, Carrie. This is for the tree. We can't eat much of it and make our tree look nice."

"Oh." Carrie looked at Janie, her little forehead wrinkled. "Mommy, why can't we eat the popcorn?"

"We can eat some," Janie reassured her. "Remember in your Christmas book, it tells about making ornaments for the tree? We're going to do that tonight."

"Me too?"

"Of course, you too," Gloria said. "It'll be a beautiful tree, with your help."

While Janie and Carrie cleaned up the supper dishes, Gloria started pushing furniture around the living room. A sofa and matching chair were the only large pieces of furniture. The sofa divided the living room from the entry. Across from it, a chair and side table sat in a cozy grouping in front of the window. A fireplace decorated one end of the room, with a small TV on a stand next to it.

"I think we should put the tree here, in front of the window," Gloria said.

"That'll look good." Janie could see the living room clearly over the bar that separated the kitchen from the rest of the apartment. "Can you move that chair by yourself?"

Gloria nodded and looked to her for instructions.

"Good. Move it over to the left, into that corner. Oh, but first, Carrie, can you push your basket out of the way?"

Carrie scampered to move a basket of toys into the middle of the floor.

"That's all right, kid, come help me with the chair. You hold the cushion."

Carrie staggered back, trying to hold the cushion although it was larger than herself while Gloria pushed the chair into the corner. In the effort to watch and hold the cushion, Carrie tripped over the basket and plopped on her bottom, cushion on top, toys scattered around her.

"Oopsy-daisy." Janie hurried around the bar, scooping up Carrie before she decided to cry. "Now we need to help Glo move the table by the chair. Here, hold this book."

When the furniture had been rearranged and Carrie's toys picked up, Gloria pulled the tree out of the box. The branches reminded Janie of the bottle brushes she'd used when Carrie was an infant.

"I bought some lights on the way home," Gloria said. "Come help me, Carrie. You can count the lights."

Gloria plugged in the string of lights to make sure they worked, and Carrie started counting. "One, two, free, four, five . . ."

Janie went to her bedroom and found her craft books in a box in the closet.

"Look at this," she said, carrying books and flyers into the living room and settling on the sofa across from the Christmas tree. "I found my patterns for scherenschnitte."

Gloria raised her eyebrows. "I hope that's a nice word."

Making a face at her roommate, Janie showed her a flyer. "It's paper ornaments. You cut them and sew them together to make them three dimensional."

Gloria peered at the instructions and shook her head. "I'm going to stick with stringing popcorn."

Janie looked at the tree, imagining the decorations already on it. "It'll be beautiful," she said.

Once the lights were on, they started making ornaments.

Janie snipped at a folded piece of paper, talking as she worked.

"If Filmore's had a portrait studio in the store, I could work there forever. I love it."

"Do you love the job or the perks?" Gloria quizzed as she pushed a needle though a piece of popcorn.

Janie looked up, frowning. "What perks?"

"That cute young Santa, that's what perks. He's a doll, judging from that portrait you painted of him."

Janie glanced at the greeting card she'd painted for

her friend. Shrugging, she tried to blow off the resemblance. "He's just Santa. Not any particular Santa."

Gloria gave her an I-know-better smile.

"Sometimes he wears a gus-dize," Carrie said, intent on stringing Fruity-Os on a piece of yarn. Most were detoured into Carrie's mouth and never made it to the string.

Janie and Gloria looked at each other, then at the little girl. Sometimes it wasn't easy figuring out what Carrie meant with her four-year-old mangling of words.

"You mean a disguise?" Gloria asked.

Carrie nodded. "He came to our house in gus-dize."

Gloria looked at Janie, unsure whether to be amused or concerned.

Janie regarded Carrie, also unsure what she was thinking.

"When was that, Carrie?"

"When the milk spilled," Carrie said.

"Which time?" Gloria and Janie asked in unison.

Then the memory of a particular milk-spill and an unwelcome guest hit Janie. "Oh. I know what she's talking about. Nick Klaus came by to apologize for getting me fired."

Gloria's eyes opened wide, and she peered around the apartment as if expecting Nick Klaus to still be there.

"To our apartment? Where was I? Why didn't you tell me about this?"

Eyes on her handwork, Janie avoided meeting Gloria's avid gaze, then shook off the wimpy attitude and lifted her chin. Why should she feel guilty? "You were at work already. It wasn't worth talking about."

"So, what's this about him being in disguise?"

"He was wearing dark glasses when he came over." As if mere dark glasses could mask that well-known face. "Carrie must've heard him say his name and came to her own conclusions."

"At least you have to admit it was nice of him to come apologize," Gloria said.

All right. Maybe she *should* feel guilty. He'd been nice and she hadn't. "It was nice," she admitted. "But it bothers me—how did he know I worked at the Honcho? Or where I lived?"

"Did you ask him?"

Janie's forehead wrinkled as she thought it through, then her cheeks warmed. "No. Things were hectic, with wiping up the milk and all. I got flustered." *Flustered, ha!* Her heart beat faster at the memory of Nick standing in her doorway, hat in hand, trying to apologize. Her instinctive response to his charm had warred with her rational side. "Come in!" one had called, while the other shouted, "Go away!"

Yeah, she'd been flustered. Returning her gaze to the paper she was cutting she concluded, "I told him to get out and stay away. I don't want strange men with bad reputations hanging around me or my daughter. Just because he's on TV doesn't mean we really know anything about him."

Gloria munched on a handful of the popcorn. "That's

true. But now you've met him in person, what do you know about him?"

Images flashed through Janie's mind: Nick protectively hovering over her in the bar, trying not to laugh at the milk spilled all over the kitchen, awed by her sketches. Nick trying his hardest to apologize and explain.

"He scares me," she whispered, more to herself than to Gloria. "He reaches out to me, and something in me wants to reach out to him, but I'm afraid."

"Afraid of Nick or afraid of the past?"

"I don't know."

Gloria wasn't going to let her get away with that. "Look, girl, the cutest guy in Texas knocks on your door and you send him away? I know you've been hurt but that's just plain insanity."

Janie's body heated up several degrees, and she glared at her friend before pointing at her daughter, intending to make the point that some things shouldn't be discussed in front of a four-year-old. Fortunately—or unfortunately— the little one was asleep, curled up beneath the tree.

"Look," she said, knowing Gloria wouldn't drop the conversation, "my experience with love and marriage wasn't all that great. It's not insanity to want to protect myself and my daughter from being hurt like that again."

"Your ex was a jerk, Janie. That's true. But not all guys are like that."

"Nick Klaus is no better. His reputation couldn't be worse. The guys at the bar certainly weren't any better. And I don't see any other men around."

Stirring the popcorn in the bowl, Gloria said, "Fine. You have all the answers. So why does Nick scare you?"

"Because he's just like—" She stopped, swallowing. Nothing could make her say her ex-husband's name. "Look, Nick's handsome and charming and everything you say. It would be easy to listen to him and believe whatever he wanted me to. But I've been there and done that and I'm not stupid enough to do it again." Rising from the sofa, she picked up Carrie and headed toward the bedroom.

After tucking the little girl into her trundle, Janie climbed onto her bed, pulling the quilt around her. Alone, she could admit it wasn't men she distrusted. It was herself. She wanted so much to trust someone, to love again, but she'd made the wrong choices before. She was older, supposedly wiser, but what was to keep her from making the same mistake?

"I won't go through that again," she whispered to her reflection in the mirror. "I have to be smarter, stronger. Even if it means I have to be alone."

Chapter Five

It was a blustery day, Janie thought, coining a phrase from one of Carrie's favorite videos. Rain slashed against the windshield. Although the wipers swished back and forth on the highest setting, most of the time Janie couldn't see well enough to make out the car in front of her. Traffic slowed to a crawl. Hopefully, she wouldn't be too late getting to work.

At last she was able to turn off onto the side roads that led her downtown to Filmore's. She had minutes to spare as she pulled into the indoor parking garage, parked, and hurried into the store.

The employee area was warm in contrast to the chill weather outside. A few people sat in the lounge, coffee cups in hand.

Ryan, one of the guys who worked unloading trucks

as new merchandise came in, greeted her. "How about some coffee?" He held out a cup and gave her an enticing grin.

"No, thanks." Janie spoke without making eye contact as she made her way past Ryan so she could change.

In the restroom, she surveyed her appearance in the mirror, tugging at her skirt, and wishing for the umpteenth time it was longer. Why couldn't she have a Mrs. Santa outfit, like Mrs. Coleman?

Mrs. Santa, she mused. In her mind's eye she pictured herself in the long red dress, a young Mrs. Santa, passing out cookies to adorable youngsters, smiling into Santa's eyes as he watched her. How would it be to be married to the most beloved man in the world? Someone kind, generous, with a quiet sense of humor . . .

She caught sight of her dreamy expression in the mirror and stopped her mental wanderings. *Get a grip!* She had to quit daydreaming about Santa. No one developed a crush on Santa Claus.

Grabbing up her street clothes, she left the restroom but found her way through the lounge blocked by Ryan.

"Ready for that cup of coffee now?" he asked.

Janie looked up at him. Ryan was good-looking and knew it. His attitude screamed "God's gift to women." Janie had heard some of the other girls talking about him. He made it a habit to try to pick up every new female employed at Filmore's.

Dredging up her stick-on smile from the Happy Honcho, she said, "It's late. I need to get to Santa-Land."

"Aw, no one's going to be in the store today. The weather's too bad. You have time to sit with us, have some coffee, and get acquainted." He glanced at the assortment of other employees in the lounge who watched the proceedings with the same attention they'd give their favorite TV program.

How could she get out of this?

"Good morning, Elf Janie, everyone." Santa leaned against the doorframe, arms crossed casually over his chest. He swept the room with his gaze, as if counting the people in the lounge rather than out on the floor.

It should've been ludicrous, being caught in the lounge by Santa Claus. Maybe it was his size, or the penetrating expression in his eyes, that made the situation anything but funny. Instead, everyone reacted as if one of the managers had walked in. Murmuring their excuses, the clerks headed back into the store.

Ryan took a seat on the sofa, smirking as he allowed Janie to walk past him to Santa's side.

"I'm glad I work in the back," he said. "We won't have another shipment coming in for about an hour. I'll stay here and keep the coffeepot company."

Glancing at Santa, Janie wondered how he'd respond to Ryan's baiting. To her surprise, he was looking at her with a concerned expression.

"Are you all right?" he asked, his voice pitched for her ears alone.

He was protecting her. The realization warmed her,

as if a candle had been lit in her heart. She gave him an imperceptible nod.

Turning away from the lounge, he offered her his arm. "Shall we go?" he asked.

Sliding her hand into the crook of his elbow, she walked with him to Santa-Land, aware of the speculative glances following them. They must look ridiculous, strolling arm in arm through the store aisles. She knew as soon as they were in Santa-Land the lounge would fill again, with this odd confrontation the topic of conversation.

She felt anything but ridiculous. She felt safe and protected.

He was a gentle giant, Janie thought, struck by another image from Carrie's supply of storybooks.

Really, she needed to get out more. Her mind was turning to mush, when everything reminded her of a children's story.

They arrived to an empty Santa-Land. Ryan had been right, the stormy weather kept early shoppers away. Nevertheless, Santa took his place on the throne, while Janie set up the photo equipment.

She checked the camera, moving it a few feet to the left and closer to Santa. The lighting was better at this angle, and the close-up shots came out clearer. She loved working with the digital camera. If the picture wasn't right, try it again without a costly waste of film. When it was right, zap it to the computer to print out. Fun and easy.

Janie realized that using the camera and computer solely for Santa pictures barely tapped the potential for gifts. She'd seen this kind of setup used to make everything from ashtrays to zany stationery. How fun it would be to experiment and come up with a completely personalized line of gifts.

The rain didn't keep the shoppers away all day. Late in the morning they arrived in full force, the kind of crowd that should make the clerks happy, keeping them busy and pulling in commissions. Although not all the clerks worked on commission, there was fierce competition among those who did. Part-timers who worked at an hourly rate were told in no uncertain terms they should wait on customers only when all the commissioned people were busy. This didn't always happen, which made for a frosty atmosphere in the breakroom some days.

Today, however, the environment was congenial, with people stopping in on their breaks while Santa and Janie, stuck in costume, ate their lunch. After finishing her cup of yogurt, Janie retrieved paper and scissors from her locker and started snipping.

"Wow, Janie, you're a real cutup," said Ryan, who was still loafing in the lounge.

Making no comment, she kept her eyes on her work until Santa asked, "What are you making?"

Knowing Ryan watched her, trying to catch her eye, she didn't look up. "Scherenschnitte."

"Gesundheit," Santa and Ryan said at the same time.

Unable to control a giggle, Janie looked up and was

surprised to see the two men glowering at each other, as if each wanted to take credit for making her laugh. Tension built between the men as they stared each other down.

"*Scherenschnitte* is German for paper-cutting," she explained, hoping to dispel the strained atmosphere invading the room. "I'm making ornaments for our Christmas tree. I learned how years ago at a workshop at the museum back home."

"That's cool," Ryan said, lifting one of the finished pieces. "Like paper snowflakes."

"Yeah, thanks." Janie frowned at him until he dropped the ornament on the table. He annoyed her. Knowing she shouldn't let him see it didn't keep her from feeling it. Guys like him—arrogant, crude, self-proclaimed studs—considered it a compliment. It gave them a feeling of power, knowing they'd gotten under her skin. She'd known a few like him in high school, and gotten to see more than her share at the Happy Honcho.

Giving her a knowing grin, he said, "Well, see ya later. Got to go back and look like I'm working."

She kept her eyes lowered until he left the room. Taking a deep breath then releasing it, she went back to snipping paper, losing herself in the task, trying to close out the rest of the world.

Santa reached across the table and picked up the ornament Ryan had dropped. "It's more involved than snowflakes," he observed. "You're very artistic, Janie."

Tension left her shoulders and she looked up, smiling.

"Thanks." His eyes held hers, and she noticed he didn't look at her with the same arrogant expression Ryan did. Santa looked interested, as if he honestly respected her talents.

She confided, "I studied art my first year in college but didn't get a chance to complete my degree." She shrugged. "I got married and had Carrie instead."

Another woman had walked in while she was speaking. "Isn't that the way it always works out?" she said. "Women have to put their lives on hold for their families all the time. That's why I'm not getting married or having kids until I launch my career."

"What career will you go into?" Janie asked.

"Fashion design. The way I see it, working in a department store like this gives me an idea what people buy, so I can design accordingly." She leaned toward Janie and lowered her voice. "But, you know, most people don't have a lick of taste. They'll buy anything as long as someone tells them it looks good."

Picking up one of Janie's ornaments, she remarked, "Cute. Have you ever thought of selling these? Handmade stuff goes over real big. Maybe you could get a booth at a flea market."

"Maybe so. I hadn't thought of that."

Janie continued snipping paper while the clerk bought a diet cola, picked up a magazine, and leafed through it between gulps of her drink. When she finished and went back into the store, Santa turned to Janie with his eyebrows raised.

"When you go back to college and get your degree, what career will launch?" he asked.

When, he said, not if. His faith in her boosted her confidence.

"I want to be a working artist. Not design, but maybe advertising or something."

"Sounds good." He winked. "Guess you can't be an elf forever, can you?"

"Right. How about you? What do you want to do when you're through being Santa?"

He shook his head. "I'm just Santa. That's all."

"Only until Christmas." Janie didn't know why she pushed the issue, since she hated when anyone pried into her life. But she felt a connection to Santa. The more they were together, the more she wanted to know about him.

He shrugged. "I'm not sure, Janie. I didn't like the guy I was before I was Santa. I'm not sure who I'll be when it's time for Santa to leave." He stood, tossing the ornament on the table. "I'll see you in Santa-Land."

"You can keep that." She felt as startled as he looked. Heat stole into her cheeks as he gazed at her a long moment before picking it up.

"Thanks," he said with a nod, then left her to put away the rest of her scherenschnitte and hurry after him to Santa-Land.

Throughout the rest of the day, she watched him through the camera lens, her artist's eye taking in every detail of his expression. For the first time, she noticed his jolly demeanor was more from his costume than from his heart. There was a seriousness in his eyes that never quite went away.

She also noticed his new manner with the children. They had been intimidated by his size before but now he spoke to each child as they approached him. In no time, he established a rapport that made it easy to take a picture but hard to get the kids to leave. They settled themselves on his lap and talked about everything, as she had shared her confidences with him during their break. He truly listened, and each child wanted to make the most of their time with him. She understood the feeling.

Finally, as the last child went off with a candy cane clutched in her hand, Santa stood stretching, while Janie put away the camera and supplies. When everything was in order, they walked to the breakroom together.

After getting her jeans and sweater from her locker, she went into the restroom to change. Without the need to rush to another job, she lingered, brushing her hair and putting on a bit of lip gloss. When she came into the breakroom after changing, she saw Santa sitting on the sofa, reading the newspaper, while a small knot of other employees discussed where they wanted to go for the evening.

Biting her lip, she hesitated, trying to decide whether to leave with the crowd or stay and talk to Santa. She'd had so much fun working with him today. However, he sat in costume, reading the newspaper as if he had nowhere else to go. In spite of the temptation to stay, if she didn't leave at the same time as everyone else she'd have to walk alone to her car. Anyone knew from watching movies or TV that parking garages were perilous places.

A tap on her shoulder startled Janie, making her shriek. Embarrassment stung her cheeks as everyone turned to look. Ryan stood beside her, laughing.

"Didn't mean to scare you," he said. "A bunch of us are going to Harry's bar for a merchandising meeting." He winked at her. "Want to come?"

Nick couldn't believe the nerve of that piece of crud, asking Janie to go barhopping with him. Bad enough Filmore's employed him to hang around without him hitting on the female employees.

But maybe Janie wanted to go out with him?

Peering at her over the newspaper, he saw the same expression on her face as he'd seen at the Honcho.

Before you got her fired.

Yeah, well, she wouldn't get fired from Filmore's. Maybe Ryan would but not Janie. Being the owner's nephew had to be good for something. He folded his newspaper, readying himself to step in.

Janie said, "I can't make it this time. Thanks for asking."

Good girl. Nick nodded to himself, some of the tension easing from his shoulders.

Ryan gave her his best big-eyed puppy-dog expression. "Please?"

Janie rolled her eyes. "You sound just like my four-year-old, always whining if she doesn't get her way."

At the words "four-year-old" Ryan backed off in a hurry. "You have a kid?"

"Yeah, would you like to see her picture?" Janie reached inside her purse.

"No. No, thanks. Gotta get going. The others are waiting." Ryan beat a retreat, joining the group waiting for him at the door leading to the garage. They passed through, leaving the back rooms empty, except for Santa and Janie.

Way to go, Nick thought, giving Janie a smile. She returned it with a shrug.

"I guess some guys don't like kids," she said.

Nick tried to think of a lighthearted rejoinder, but nothing came to mind. He sat, gazing at her like an idiot, content with her company.

Silence echoed around them, the feeling of emptiness from the store filtering into the employees' lounge.

"I need to go," Janie said, staying put, casting a worried glance at the door to the parking garage. Taking a deep breath, she gave a small laugh and said, "Parking garages give me the creeps. Could I wait for you to change and then . . . could you walk me to my car?"

She rushed through the last part of her request, a blush staining her cheeks.

"Yes," he said.

YES! He mentally spiked a ball in the end zone.

No! The image froze as he realized the full implications.

He couldn't change clothes unless he was ready to tell her right here, right now, he was Nick Klaus.

Wouldn't that go over big. She'd probably scream and run straight into Ryan's arms.

A desperate idea blossomed in his mind.

"I don't have to change. Mr. Filmore has asked me to do some promotional spots for the store after hours." *Don't ask where,* he pleaded mentally. He'd find some way to get back into the building and leave his costume later. He offered her his arm as he'd done that morning, saying, "Shall we?"

She smiled and took his arm.

They left the store, pulling the locked door shut, as per the agreement Nick had with the security guard. In unspoken consent, they hurried to her car, the sound of their footsteps echoing off the concrete walls. If this were a movie, a car would come screeching around the corner, racing straight for them. Or—another scenario from the movies—someone would be lurking in the back seat with a large knife. Nick gave the back seat a quick once-over to dispel that fear while she unlocked and opened the door.

She got in and locked the door, waving at him, then cracked the window. "I'll wait for you to get in your car, if you want."

"Yeah, thanks." He paused, grinning at her, although

she probably couldn't see it through the beard. He lingered by her door, trying to draw out their time together. "See you tomorrow."

"Yeah." She smiled back at him.

He felt her eyes on him as he walked to his car. Because he arrived at work early, his car was parked closer to the entrance of the store. Not a top-of-the-line sports car like the one that had ended up wrapped around a light pole, but an old muscle car. His first car. Like a worn security blanket, it went with him from home to college to the pros to the present. He got in on the driver's side, turned the key in the ignition . . . *click. Click-click. Click.*

Dead battery.

He looked over at Janie, who lifted her eyebrows, questioning.

Nick shrugged and got out. "Dead battery. Do you have jumper cables?"

"Sure. I'll pull my car around."

It didn't take long to get the cars in position and the jumpers set up. Janie knew her way around a battery.

"My dad used to drill me on this kind of thing," she said. "I had to be able to use the jumper cables, check the fluids, and change a tire before he let me drive anywhere alone."

With her engine idling, she attached the cables to her battery while he held the other end.

"Okay," she said, after the cables were attached to her engine. "Go ahead and connect them to your battery."

Nick looked at how the red and black ends were attached to Janie's battery, trying to recall the facts and physics of jumper cables.

"Positive goes to negative," he muttered, reaching toward his engine.

"No!" Janie yanked his arm before he could touch the cable end to his battery, causing him to lose his grip. Sparks flew as the ends of the cable hit the side of the car. Janie took the cables, holding the ends by their rubber grips.

"You'll ruin your battery that way," she said, with a smile. "Positive goes to positive, not negative."

"Positive goes to negative," Nick protested.

"That's magnets, not batteries. Opposites attract. In magnets, the positive end and the negative end are attracted to each other. Like ends repel each other. It's easy to get mixed up." She grinned suddenly, showing him a paper attached to the jumper cables. "Whenever I get the jumper cables out, I read the directions to make sure."

Turning away, she bent over and attached the cables to his battery.

Nick watched, his brain whirling. Attract. Repel. Opposites. Sparks. *Oh, yes, definitely sparks,* he thought, gazing at her as she straightened. As if male and female weren't opposite enough, she was small, leaning against the side of his car. Her head barely reached his shoulder. Small, soft, sweet.

As if she felt the attraction too, she faced him, standing so close, leaning closer . . .

"Try starting your car now," she said, shifting away as if giving him room to get by. But Nick saw her sideways glance, the trembling in her hands. She'd felt it, too, the electricity that arched between them as it did from her car to his.

He got into his car and turned the ignition, glad when it caught. Best let the engines run for a bit and charge the dead battery. Getting out of the car, he walked to her side, where she looked at the engines of the cars as if they needed constant supervision.

"I guess winter finally got here," Janie said, making nervous conversation while hugging her arms against the chill breeze that blew through the garage. They were far enough toward the center that the rain couldn't get to them, but the north wind whistled in and around the concrete pillars. "Texas weather is the pits. You never know from day to day what season to dress for."

Nick said, "Are you cold? I have a jacket in my car."

She shook her head. "I'm fine. Thanks."

Even so, Nick moved closer to her, trying to shelter her from the wind. Again, as if drawn by an irresistible force, she shifted toward him, then abruptly pulled herself a few steps away.

"There's your problem," she said, pointing between the cars.

Taking a step back, he squinted, trying to see what she meant. "What is?"

She stepped to his side, directing his attention to the

front of his car. "See? Your lights were on. I'll bet you left them on this morning."

He turned toward her, smiling. "I'll bet you're right."

Gazing into her eyes for a heartbeat, Nick gave into the magnetic attraction of opposites and bent toward her.

She smelled fresh, like springtime. His lips brushed hers. Ah, so sweet. He kissed her again, putting his hands on her waist and drawing her closer. She held back at first, then sighed, her lips parting beneath his.

Without warning, she struggled in his embrace, pushing at him until he stepped away.

" 'Tchoo!" She turned her face barely in time to keep from sneezing into his beard.

The stupid, ticklish, angel-hair beard.

" 'Tchoo!" Janie rubbed her nose, leaving it slightly pinker than her cheeks.

He chuckled and reached for her hands—

They both heard it at the same time: the roar of an engine getting louder as it came toward them. Janie gasped and stepped into his arms, letting him hold her and shield her from the threat coming up the ramps of the garage.

The yellow light revolving on the top of the car washed over the concrete walls, making them pulsate amber and white. The security officer drove up to them, laughing.

"This beats all," he said. "Having some trouble with your sleigh, Santa?"

Janie moved out of his arms. Clearing her throat, she said, "I think we've let the battery charge long enough."

"It's taken care of, officer," Nick said.

"Don't need any help? Those jumper cables can be tricky sometimes."

Nick leaned over and disengaged the cables. His car purred under its own power. Slamming down the hood, he nodded at the officer. "She'll do. Thanks for stopping."

Would the man take the hint?

He did and drove off with a wave.

Janie rolled up the jumper cables, slammed down the hood of her car, then hesitated, looking at him with a slight smile. "It's gotten late," she said. "I need to get on home."

Nick caught her hand, not wanting the moment to end. Something had started here, something big and new. Something he didn't want to go away.

Their fingers twined together. He drew her closer and kissed her cheek. "I'll see you tomorrow, then. Good night, Janie."

In the dim light, he saw her cheeks flare with color. Gently removing her hand from his grasp, she whispered "good night," then hurried to her car.

He watched her drive away, then went through the motions of spiking a ball.

"Yes!"

Chapter Six

Later that night, Janie and Gloria sat together in the living room. Janie put finishing touches on a wreath for the door, while Gloria lounged with her feet up, channel surfing.

Paper angels, snowflakes, trees, and candles were interspersed among the greenery, held in place with blobs of hot glue. Her mind on earlier events, Janie's hands were on automatic pilot, shooting glue, sticking paper, shooting glue, sticking paper.

Santa had kissed her.

She'd kissed him back.

That was so totally unlike her.

But it was so sweet, so . . . wonderful.

When she'd gotten home, she opened the trunk of her car and gazed at the jumper cables. An aura of magic surrounded them, just as it had seemed to surround her and Santa in the parking garage.

Santa. Grimacing, she shook her head. She should know the name of the man who kissed her.

He'd told her, but she wasn't sure he'd told her the truth. When had she ever met someone named Nicodemus before?

She tried saying it under her breath. "Nicodemus."

"What?"

Shaken out of her reverie, Janie blinked at Gloria, then made a quick recovery.

"What do you think?" she asked, holding up the wreath.

Gloria took the wreath from Janie, admiring the tiny paper ornaments interspersed among the greenery. "That's great. You have such a knack for decorating. The whole apartment looks Christmasy, thanks to you."

Colored lights glowed around each window, and an arrangement of candles and greenery added scent and color on the mantel. Lights on the bottle-brush tree twinkled amid the paper and popcorn ornaments. All of Carrie's strings of Fruity-Os had already been nibbled away, leaving bright strands of yarn on the lower branches.

Janie unplugged the glue gun and put away her supplies. "Do you know of any flea markets around here?"

Gloria shrugged. "No. Not anywhere close. Why?"

"A girl at work said she thought I could sell the scherenschnitte ornaments at a flea market."

Gloria regarded her a moment, tapping her fingers

against the arm of the sofa. "Do you have a lot already made?"

"I have about fifty extra. I wasn't sure how many our tree would take. I kind of got started on them and didn't stop."

"I know." Glo laughed, wrinkling her nose. "I've been vacuuming little paper scraps for days. But selling the extra ornaments is a good idea. How about I take a few to the salon and see if any of our clients are interested?"

"That'd be great. Are you sure it's all right with your boss?"

"Oh, yeah, we get stuff in all the time. A lot of it's not as nice as your ornaments."

"Thanks." Janie yawned and stretched. "I'm going to bed now. I have to work the early shift tomorrow."

"With which Santa?"

Janie made a face at her roommate and went to the larger of the two bedrooms where Carrie was already sleeping. She'd tucked the little one in much earlier, so the room was dim and quiet. Light gleamed around the edges of the bathroom door. Carrie slept in her trundle bed, curled up in a ball around BeBe Bunny with the covers kicked off. Janie pulled the quilt over her, then turned back the covers on her own bed before going into the bathroom.

She washed her face, flossed her teeth, changed into the long, worn T-shirt she wore at night, then climbed into her bed. Sitting with her arms looped around her knees, she looked at Carrie and smiled. Reaching down, she stroked the little girl's curls with one finger, marveling at the softness of her hair, the perfection of the sturdy little body. Carrie had helped her understand what real love was. Committed. Unconditional. Forever.

That's what she wanted from a man. Next time she fell in love . . .

Would she ever? Was there truly someone out there for her?

A vision of Santa came into her mind—the way he'd looked at her when they talked about her career. So much of his face was obscured by the beard, but his eyes had held the light of admiration. For her, a single mom with a high school diploma who didn't even have a decent job.

Was it wrong to think about him like this? That maybe, just maybe, the friendship between them could grow, could—

Whoa. This was too weird. Every time she thought about Santa, it was as Santa, not as a guy dressed up in a Santa suit.

"Get out of the fantasy world," she whispered. "Santa isn't really Santa." She reached over to set the alarm. Santa was a guy dressed up, playing a part. It's that guy who'll be around after Christmas.

And I want to keep seeing him after Christmas.

The realization sent goosebumps up her arms and a panicky shiver down her spine.

Did she really want to pursue a relationship? Was he the right one?

She wouldn't know until she met the man himself. Not Santa but Nicodemus. Face to face, without the beard.

How could she do that?

Ask him out. It's what Gloria would do.

"I can't do that," she whispered.

Then you'll never know, the inner voice taunted.

Turning on her side, she watched the digital numbers of her alarm clock change, counting minute by endless minute. This was going to be a long night.

The obnoxious buzz of the alarm clock didn't send ice picks of pain through Nick's skull the way it used to. Sobriety had its benefits. No more hangovers.

No pain meant it was easy to drift back to sleep . . .

Nick had no idea what jerked him awake. Breathing hard, as if he'd been running, he looked at the clock and his heart rate went up another level.

Late.

Late! He wrestled his way out of bed, dashing to the shower. Only half-awake, he dressed, grabbing up jeans and a pullover from the clean clothes pile. For the final touch, he pulled his cap low and slid his shades on—his usual disguise until he could get to the store and put on the Santa suit.

He made it to Filmore's in record time due to every light being green. Maybe there was something to be said for prayer. According to his watch, he was early for his shift, hopefully early enough that no one would be in the breakroom. He'd just have to run for it and hope—maybe even try that praying stuff again—that no one recognized him before he got in costume.

Halfway between his car and the door, another car swept into the garage and parked by his.

A quick backward glance revealed Janie, getting out of her car.

Had she seen him get out of Santa's car?

Heart pounding, Nick kept his back to her and forced his feet to move toward the entrance to the store. A car door slammed shut and her footsteps sounded behind him, quick and light. Was that her breathing he heard? As if she, too, were late for work and hurrying to punch in.

She was near, right behind him. Every nerve on his body signaled her approach, zinging into awareness. He remembered her body in his arms, the touch of her lips on his.

He remembered the cute way she sneezed when his beard tickled her nose.

His beard. *Oh, no.*

He couldn't let her see him like this.

Covering his mouth with one hand, he grabbed for the door, making retching noises. Out of the corner of his eye, he saw Janie, hand out to open the door, an expression of concern on her face.

"Are you all right?" she asked.

In reply, Nick pushed past her into the store, heading straight for the breakroom, his hands still covering his mouth. With the cap, the sunglasses, and a heavy jacket covering his body, no one should be able to recognize him.

Relief broke through the haze of fake nausea when he saw no one in the breakroom. Still, he kept his hands over his mouth until he made it safely into the restroom and locked the door. Leaning against it, he wondered if his symptoms were actually fake. His heart pounded and a cold sweat covered his body.

"That was too close," he told his image in the mirror.

Way too close. The upshot was that he was stuck in the restroom, probably for the rest of the day. He already heard people moving around in the breakroom.

"What's going on?" he heard a woman say.

"I think Santa's sick." Janie's voice.

Okay. In five minutes or so, the entire store would know Santa was sick in the employee restroom. So he wouldn't be able to stay in here all day. He had to get out. Could he finesse his way out so no one would recognize Nick Klaus?

Finesse? Yeah, right. Just like he'd done getting in here, retching all the way. That's finesse.

Listening at the door, he couldn't tell how many people were in the breakroom. The store opened at ten. He and Janie were supposed to be in Santa-Land at 10:30. He looked at his watch: 10:25.

Grabbing a handful of paper towels, he held them over his mouth, covering the lower part of his face. Count of three, open the door.

Janie was there, in costume. A female clerk sat at the

table, sipping coffee. Both looked at him as he left the room.

"I'm sick. Gotta go home," he said, avoiding looking at either of them directly. He headed toward the door to the parking lot.

Footsteps behind him.

"Santa?" Janie's voice. "Is there anything I can do to help?"

Just shoot me, he thought. Here was the sweetest woman in the world offering her help even though, for all she knew, he was sick as a dog. The fact that she disliked him, except as Santa, made the sick stomach a reality.

"Santa?" A pause. Coming up close behind him, she laid a hand on his shoulder. "Nicodemus? Can I help?"

"No. I'll be all right." He couldn't look at her. If he did, he'd be lost. Pulling away, he left the building and headed for the sanctuary of his car.

The store was empty this morning, with very few early shoppers. Clerks huddled together, gossiping, as Janie walked through the store on her way to the manager's office to report Santa's illness.

The sound of heels clicking a no-nonsense cadence brought the clerks to attention. Everyone took pains to look as busy as they could with no one to wait on as a woman in a suit approached the area. Janie recognized Ms. Garza, the floor manager.

"Janie, Santa just called in sick," she said when she

reached her side. "Mr. Hopkins won't be able to come in until this afternoon. If you'll stay until he gets here, I'd appreciate it. Of course, you'll be paid for your time."

"Thank you. Of course I'll stay."

"I was afraid that young Santa wouldn't work out," Ms. Garza murmured, more to herself than to Janie. "But Mr. Filmore insisted he'd be fine."

"He's very good," Janie said. "He probably has that stomach virus that's been going around. As much as he deals with the kids, it's a wonder he hasn't been sick before this."

Ms. Garza sighed. "I guess you're right." Sweeping a glance around the area, empty of people except for themselves and the sales clerks, she said, "It doesn't make much difference, does it? You'd hardly know it's Christmas at this store."

Not knowing what to say to this, Janie nodded. Ms. Garza took this as encouragement to continue.

"What we need is a reason for people to come downtown to Filmore's. Do you know what I mean?"

Janie nodded again, her heart pounding. This was the opportunity she'd been looking for. "I think what Filmore's needs is a photo studio. But not just for portraits and that kind of thing. With this equipment, the digital camera and the computer, we could design anything. Flyers. Advertising brochures. Business cards. Everything personalized. We sell things like briefcases and computers. What if we offered our services in completely outfitting a businessman or woman? They could buy everything from their business cards to their suits right here in Filmore's."

Ms. Garza stared at her so long Janie felt like she'd sprouted horns from her head.

"I like that," she said, finally. "I really like that. I'll talk it over with Mr. Filmore the first chance I get. Of course, it'll be too late to save Christmas. And it'd take some remodeling. Thank you, Janie." She left, the wheels in her head obviously spinning as she made her way back to her office.

Janie watched her go, pleased at the reception of her idea. Then it dawned on her she'd never get credit for it. Ms. Garza would present it to Mr. Filmore. Even if the idea was put into practice, it didn't guarantee Janie a job. She was still just a picture-taking elf, with not many more days 'til Christmas and the end of this job.

Shrugging, she went to the breakroom, hoping to find a newspaper full of want ads.

Nick moved his car to the parking garage in the building next to Filmore's and walked into the building. Most people didn't know that Nicodemus "Fil" Filmore had his offices next door to his downtown department store. It was generally thought, if anyone thought about it at all, that the Filmore family, owner of several department stores and buildings, didn't dirty its hands with being involved directly in the business. That wasn't how Uncle Fil worked. He might not walk through the stores every day or even every week, but his managers knew what he looked like and who he was. He spoke with them every day on the phone and had biweekly meetings. His only other sibling, Nick's mother, took no interest in the business except to bank her dividends.

When Nick received his sentence, Uncle Fil had pulled every string available to get his namesake into the store. Nick needed to be gainfully employed, especially since being fired from the TV studio. Uncle Fil had come through for him. In fact, Uncle Fil had been the only one from Nick's family to stand by him during the ordeal of his hearing. Even though Nick realized the old guy's main interest was to get him into the family business, he still appreciated his help and support.

He could use some of that family support now. Maybe Uncle Fil could help him figure out this mess.

He liked Janie. Admired her courage in taking on the world by herself. She did the right things, the good things.

She liked Santa.

She despised Nick.

On second thought, no one could help him figure this one out.

Personal problems aside, there were some things he'd been wanting to discuss with Uncle Fil. Every day he spent in the store, he was confronted with some sorry attitudes from employees, lax protocol, inefficiency. Although Uncle Fil made every effort to stay on top of things, there was a lot his managers didn't report.

When Nick was admitted into his office, Uncle Fil

rose and came around his massive desk. The small man's bald head gleamed with pleasure as he shook Nick's hand.

"Good to see you, son, how is everything?"

"Hi, Uncle Fil. Things are going fine with me." Besides being confused as all get out. "I'm doing all right, but your team's in trouble."

Fil returned to his seat behind the desk and rested his elbows on the polished expanse, his fingers steepled. "My team?"

Nick sat in one of the upholstered chairs before the desk and tilted it so it balanced on its back legs.

"Filmore's. They're not pulling together, you know?"

Uncle Fil dropped his hands to his desk and sighed. "No, I don't know what you're talking about, Nick. Could you drop the sports analogies and tell me straight out?"

Nick brought the chair back onto all four legs. "This is hard for me, Uncle Fil. I've been doing a lot of thinking lately. And listening. And the scuttlebutt is, Filmore's Downtown is the last place on earth anyone wants to shop."

Uncle Fil's eyebrows climbed up his forehead. "What do you mean, no one wants to shop at Filmore's? We have the best sales figures in the state. We employ more people, we give more to charity—"

"Right. Because the other stores and your other business interests pull this one along. I'm not talking about Filmore's the corporation, but Filmore's the store."

Fil settled back in his chair. "I'm listening."

"People don't come downtown to shop anymore. That may be obvious but the store hasn't made any changes to accommodate that."

"We have a store in every major mall in the area."

"But you're stuffing the same kind of merchandise into this downtown store that you have in the malls. The same kind of people don't shop here. Do you know who you see on the sidewalks outside?"

Uncle Fil shuddered. "I don't go outside if I can help it."

Nick grinned. He knew Uncle Fil wasn't really a snob, just a scared little man. "It's not so bad. There are a lot of businessmen, just like you. And women too. Travelers on business at conventions, staying in the hotels around here. The way I see it, you're sitting on a goldmine, having the only retail store around. But you have to stock it with stuff for them, not for the suburbanites in their mini-vans and SUVs."

Uncle Fil pulled a yellow legal pad toward him and picked out his favorite pen from the set arrayed on the desk. "Go on. What kind of things should we stock?"

"For one thing, you don't need as many clothes. All you need is stuff for the business traveler. You know, suits. Some sportswear for golfing or sightseeing. Things they can pick up if they forgot to pack it, or something special for an unexpected event."

Uncle Fil nodded and scribbled on the paper, the black ink making bold marks. "If we cater to the business traveler, we don't have to carry housewares. No more mixers or breadmakers."

"Right. But you do want electronic gadgets. Anything handheld or portable."

Uncle Fil nodded and added more lines. "Calculators. Palm-size computers. Laptops."

"Games." Nick grinned. "Don't forget the games."

Uncle Fil wrote as he talked. "And Filmore's could work with the hotels. Woo the concierge. That's who makes recommendations."

"You're already ahead of me," Nick said, standing. "My work here is done."

Uncle Fil waved him back into the chair. "Sit down, son. Stay a few more minutes. Tell me, what can we do to boost our Christmas sales?"

Nick shrugged. "I don't know. What do you usually do?"

"Decorate." Uncle Fil stippled dots on the margin of his tablet, his brow wrinkled. "Santa Claus pictures. Sales." He heaved a sigh. "But nothing has struck any interest. Probably because, as you say, anyone can get these things at any of our stores. For downtown, we need something new. Something exclusive."

Nick sat at the edge of his chair, his eyes on the carpet, shaking his head. What was he doing here? He was just an ex–drugged-out jock. He didn't understand business.

"Brainstorm with me, son. What do we have at Filmore's Downtown that no one else has?"

Janie.

She was so much on his mind and in his heart, he thought for a second he'd spoken her name aloud. But Uncle Fil didn't react as if he'd heard anything, just continued looking at him as if he had something to offer.

She had so much to give, so much talent and creativity . . .

"Let me show you something," he said. He pulled his wallet out of his pocket and showed his uncle the scherenschnitte angel Janie had given him.

Uncle Fil held the delicate item and gave a low whistle. "This is beautifully done. What's your idea?"

"The girl who takes pictures of the kids with Santa makes these. Could she sell them here? One of the other girls suggested she take it to a flea market. If these would sell at a flea market, why not here?"

It wasn't much of a plan. In fact, it was no plan at all, but Uncle Fil appeared fascinated. He did something Nick had never seen him do before. He leaned back in his chair, balancing on the back legs. Eyes on the ceiling, he said, "An exclusive. Unique. No two alike. Handmade. Oh, my boy, these will go over big."

"I've seen some of her other work too," Nick continued. "She paints portraits, incredible stuff."

Bringing his chair back to the ground, Uncle Fil grinned at Nick and asked, "What are your plans for after Christmas?"

Nick shrugged. The same question had haunted him

for days but he hadn't come up with any answers. His agent hadn't called with anything new. "I don't know."

"Think about this—stay on at Filmore's. We won't need a Santa Claus, but we do have a place for Nick Klaus."

Nick shook his head. "Nick Klaus is just a retired jock with a bum knee. No one needs him."

"That's where you're wrong, son. There will be big changes at Downtown Filmore's after the new year. I just got off the phone with Ms. Garza. She had a dynamite idea about having a portrait and printing studio. It falls right in line with this appealing to the businessperson format. But you know me, Nick. I don't travel. I don't like to get out. There aren't many people I can trust to keep me filled in on what's actually going on."

Pleasure filled Nick at the thought of being wanted— more, of being needed. But old habits die hard, especially habits of thought. "I'm not the right person for this, Uncle Fil. You want Quinn, someone with actual business experience."

"Nick, if I'd wanted Quinn I'd have hired him years ago. You said it yourself, your days as a jock are over. Start thinking of yourself as Nick Klaus, entrepreneur."

Entrepreneur. It sounded good.

It was hard going home after the interview with Uncle Fil, hard to settle to anything. He missed the sense of direction that came from having a job, the daily schedule and deadlines. He wandered around his house, peering into the spacious rooms. He couldn't think of it as home. He'd had the place built on the recommendation of his investment manager, who'd gotten all excited about the ritzy location, where other celebrities lived. This house was somebody's dream of perfection, but not Nick's.

Finally, he went into the one room he'd designed himself, the gym. This was the only place in the house where he felt completely at home. Thinking back over other places he'd lived—the dorms and apartments of college, the hotel rooms on the road—he wondered exactly what it was he missed. Piles of dirty clothes? Nah, he still had those, although they were picked up and cleaned by the maid who came twice a week. The clutter of magazines and papers? Nope. Still had those, too, although not as cluttered, since the same maid took care of that. Thinking of the people he employed—the maid, the cook, the gardener—made him realize the thing he missed was being surrounded by other people. Not employees but friends and comrades.

Chalk up another first. First time in years sober, first time working with his uncle, first time alone.

When he'd been drunk or high, the alone part never bothered him. Now, the quiet and solitude were giving him the willies. He had to get out of here and around people. Now.

After showering, he grabbed his keys and headed out the door. Another stipulation of his probation was two hundred hours of community service. It was high time he got to it.

He ended up playing Santa.

The costume was brushed cotton rather than velvet, but it was as effective as a disguise. Standing by a kettle and ringing a bell outside another Filmore's at one of the malls, he got a firsthand look at who shopped and how much they bought. It didn't seem right, doing community service and market research at the same time.

After an hour, he was relieved by two church ladies, geared up for their stint at bell-ringing.

"Oh, I love your costume. You look so authentic," one said.

The other appraised his appearance with the eye of an expert. "Do you have an opening the evening of the nineteenth? That's when our church is having its children's program. There will be punch and cookies afterward, and it would be sweet to have a visit from Santa. If you don't charge too much, that is."

With his mind on the importance of generosity and giving, there was only one thing he could reply.

"No charge, ladies. Just tell me when and where and I'll be there."

In his car, he hesitated before heading home. Here he was, all dressed up and nowhere to go. At a stoplight, he drummed his fingers on the steering wheel as he considered his options. Who would want to see Santa Claus?

The light changed, and he turned, heading toward Children's Medical Center.

Chapter Seven

"Janie, your cut-paper ornaments are flying off the tree at the salon," Gloria told her at breakfast a couple of days later. Or what passed for breakfast. Janie and Gloria started each day with a diet shake. Carrie was the only one who actually ate breakfast. Today it was mouse-shaped pancakes and chocolate milk.

Janie asked, "Should I make some more? It's my day off. I have plenty of time to cut up."

"Is it a mommy day?" asked Carrie.

"Sure is, pumpkin. What do you want to do today?"

Gloria reached over and ran her fingers through Carrie's curls. "Why don't you bring her to the salon and let me style her hair? Then you can dress her up and take her to see Santa." With a sly wink, she added, "I can style your hair too. Got to look good for Santa."

Heat rose to Janie's cheeks. Avoiding Gloria's eyes, she said, "That's a good idea. It'll be nice to have a portrait of Carrie with Santa."

"All right. Come in about an hour from now. I have an opening then."

"We'll be there."

Gloria finished off her diet shake, then grabbed her purse and keys, and headed out the door. "See you later."

"Looks like it's just you and me, kid." Janie tweaked Carrie's nose. "Are you excited about going to see Santa?"

Carrie gave a vigorous nod, her mouth too full of pancakes to speak.

So am I. She loved spending the day with Carrie but had started looking forward to the time with Santa. His sick day had thrown off their schedule, and she missed being with him.

Working with him, she corrected herself.

Not only had his illness disrupted their schedule, it had torpedoed her plans to ask him out.

As if she'd have enough guts to do that, anyway.

It wasn't a matter of courage. It needed to be done. The sooner she got to know the real man—

What if she didn't like the real man?

Oh, this is ridiculous! Of course I'll like him. A person doesn't change themselves by changing clothes.

Aaauugh!

Trying to get her thoughts in order, she asked Carrie,

"What are you going to ask Santa to bring you for Christmas?"

Carrie shrugged her shoulders. "I'da know."

"Would you like him to bring you some surprises?"

Carrie nodded, curls bobbing. "I like surprises."

"Me too."

"Is Santa Claus your friend?" Carrie regarded Janie with wide-eyed interest, a chocolate-milk mustache over her mouth.

"Yes, he is." Janie smiled at the thought. A four-year-old's idea of friendship was so different from an adult's. At four, a friend was someone your own size, someone to play with. For herself, who knew where friendship might lead?

She sipped her diet shake, musing about her relationship with Santa. It was frustrating. What did he look like without his costume? And his name—Nicodemus—was that real or just something to make her laugh? Jolly old Saint Nicodemus. Jolly, maybe. But old didn't fit into it at all.

No, he was young and kind. Protective. Smiling, she remembered how he gave Ryan the eye when he flirted with her. Santa didn't flirt that way. He was respectful.

What was his story? From what she could tell, he was old enough to have a full-time career, not just a part-time, seasonal job. She could be wrong, but he didn't seem like a college student on the lookout for a few extra bucks.

"I'm froo." Carrie pushed her plate away. Janie put it

in the sink and attempted to wipe up the stickiness from the table and from Carrie's hands.

"You're going to need a bath before we go see Gloria."

"Nuh-uh." Slipping from her chair, Carrie ran from the kitchen to the living room. "Can't catch me!"

"Carrie, come back here. We don't have time." Janie went to the living room, wearing her stern mother look with her hands on her hips.

Carrie giggled and crawled under the end table.

In spite of everything, they arrived at the salon on time.

While there, Carrie was an angel for Gloria, sitting still when asked. But when released from the chair, she darted around underfoot until Janie had to set her on a time-out in an unused chair. Carrie pouted a while, making faces at herself in the mirror, her finger in her mouth. Finally, she fell asleep.

"She hasn't outgrown her morning nap," Janie said as Gloria shampooed her hair. It felt heavenly: the warm water flowing through her hair, her friend's fingers massaging peach-scented shampoo into her scalp, and then the warm water taking the suds away.

"Don't fall asleep on me," Gloria said. "You're getting a faraway look in your eyes."

"I bet you see that a lot. Having my hair washed seems like the ultimate luxury."

Gloria trimmed Janie's hair, then styled it. As she watched the transformation in the mirror, Janie wished she had a marketable skill like Gloria. In her hands, Janie's hair took on a whole new look.

"Wow," Janie said. "I don't look like I'm in high school anymore."

"I've been waiting forever to get you in here. Your hair was cute the other way but this look is a little more sophisticated."

"As befits an artiste." Gloria's boss, Tina, had come into the room. "Do you want your commission in cash or check?" she asked.

Janie raised her eyebrows, the only part of her that could move while Gloria held her captive with a hot curling iron.

"What commission?" she asked.

"On your little doilies," Tina said.

Janie's eyes widened. "I didn't see the ornaments when I came in."

"That's because we sold out yesterday. I hope you don't mind but I'm keeping ten percent of each one sold."

"Sure. How much did you sell them for?"

"Five dollars."

Janie eyed Gloria in the mirror. Glo looked as smug as if she'd swallowed the canary.

"That's expensive," she hissed at her friend.

"People paid it," Gloria hissed back. "And it's worth it. I know how much work goes into those things."

Tina came back in the room and set a check on the dressing table in front of Janie.

Janie's vision blurred. People had bought her ornaments! She'd actually made money from her art. A dream come true.

She couldn't wait to tell Santa.

Another day in Santa-Land with Big Mama in attendance.

Nick grimaced. It was his own fault. He'd thrown the schedule off when he called in sick earlier in the week. There had been no way he could've worked with Janie that day. Even though he checked the schedule to see when they would be together again, he wasn't sure he'd be able to face her even then.

His conscience bothered him. She didn't know that Santa was Nick Klaus. Their friendship wasn't based on truth.

How was he going to look her in the eye tomorrow and the days after that, feeling what he did for her and not tell her the truth? How could he explain the truth to her? Now that he was out of the limelight and sober, *he* even liked Santa better than Nick Klaus.

A desperate scheme perked in his mind as he imagined going through the rest of his life as Santa, never revealing his true identity. After all, Superman did it. But Superman's costume wasn't seasonal.

"Hi, Santa!"

Nick looked up and saw Carrie jumping up and down and waving at him from behind the velvet barrier.

"Hi, Carrie! Come on over."

Janie came up behind Carrie, absolutely gorgeous in a red sweater and jeans. She looked different somehow, more beautiful.

"It doesn't look very busy today," she said. Carrie climbed into his lap and squeezed his neck in a hug that almost knocked off his whiskers. He managed to keep them on, settle Carrie on his lap, and smile at Janie all at the same time.

Janie stood and smiled back.

He couldn't look at her without remembering how she felt in his arms. His feelings must've showed on his face. When she bent toward him, his eyelids lowered, anticipating the soft sweetness of her lips on his . . . then he had to sit there like a fool when she straightened Carrie's dress and tweaked her hair around her face.

"I'd better get out of the way and let Mrs. Coleman take the picture," Janie said. "I'm worse than the other moms." Stepping out of the way, Janie waved at Big Mama.

Nick pointed toward the camera, showing Carrie where to look.

"Smile, now. There are a lot of people who want a picture of a pretty girl like you," he said.

Carrie giggled. "Mommy paints pictures. I do too."

"I've seen some of your mommy's pictures. I haven't seen any of yours. Will you paint a picture for me, Carrie?"

"Uh huh. I'll draw you a big Christmas tree."

"All right. That'll be a nice present for Santa. What do you want for Christmas?"

"You can bring me a surprise," Carrie said, busy stroking the soft plush suit.

Ms. Garza came swishing up in her power suit and high heels. "Janie. Good. I'd heard you were in the store. Could you come to my office, please?" Without waiting for acquiescence, she turned on her heel and walked away.

"What's that all about?" Janie wondered aloud.

"You go on," Nick told her. "Carrie can stay here with us until you get back."

"Of course, she can," Mrs. Coleman chimed in. "Go on, Janie. You can't ignore a summons like that."

She couldn't ignore it, but she didn't like it. Her stomach fluttering, she wondered what she could've possibly done to be called into the office. Thank God she was dressed in jeans and a sweater instead of her elf costume. She couldn't take herself seriously in the costume and didn't believe management could either.

Following in Ms. Garza's wake made her the center of attention of all the clerks they walked by. She could imagine the gossip in the breakroom over this.

When they got to Ms. Garza's office, Janie was surprised to see a small bald man there. Ms. Garza launched into a spiel without making introductions.

"Janie, your talents have come to our attention," Ms. Garza said. "Your work with the photography is excellent. We've also discovered you're an artist." As she said this, she picked up a scherenschnitte angel from her desk. "I understand you also draw and paint."

Janie nodded, unsure what this was all about.

"We have a proposition for you," the bald man said.

Janie looked at him blankly.

"I'm sorry, let me introduce myself. I'm Fil Filmore."

Owner of the Filmore's chain of department stores.
Janie felt faint. *What's going on?*

"The proposition we have is this—you give Filmore's exclusive right to these paper decorations. You'll make them, we'll market them as a one-of-a-kind, nowhere-but-here item."

Janie blinked.

Mr. Filmore continued. "As a Filmore's artist in residence, you will receive a salary—it'll be less than our salespeople, Ms. Langston—and a commission on each piece of work you sell, based on the cost of the item. I'm sure some of these things are bigger or more time consuming, so would cost more. But the point we want to make, this is a Filmore's exclusive, only found here at the downtown store. Our mall stores will not have these. Does that sound good to you, young lady?"

Sound good? It sounded like a dream come true.

Except . . .

"I'm afraid I don't have any ornaments made right now," she said. "I sold them at a salon where a friend works. I can make some more . . ."

Mr. Filmore waved away her concern. "That's where the artist in residence bit comes in. You set up your own workspace and make them on the premises. Let people watch. That way they'll be more likely to buy. Filmore's will get you all the supplies you need. If you don't mind coming in early tomorrow, about eight o'clock, we can get started on your studio. I want you here to tell maintenance what you need and how you want it set up. You can start as soon as the studio is done."

"Thank you. I'll be here."

Janie left the office and stood in the foyer, dazed. How had this happened? One minute she was looking through want ads for another low-paying job, the next, she was an artist.

"Oh, Janie, still here?" Ms. Garza came up behind her, all smiles. "I know this isn't exactly what we talked about but it's a start, isn't it?" Lowering her voice, she confided, "And Mr. Filmore's told me about some other plans in the works for the new year. It's going to be exciting here at Downtown Filmore's."

"How did Mr. Filmore find out about the scherenschnitte?"

"He knows everything that goes on. He's got his finger on the pulse of this and all the other Filmore's stores." Her pager went off. Glancing at it, she said, "I have to go. Congratulations, Janie. This looks like the jump start of a whole new career for you."

A career in art. Just like she'd told Santa.

Leaving the office area, she headed to Santa-Land, the sound of her footsteps on the tile picking up speed as she neared it.

She'd recognized the scherenschnitte angel. Sure,

several people had seen her cutting the ornaments but she'd given away only one—to Santa.

Who better to "jump-start" her career as an artist?

He came into view standing behind the ropes in Santa-Land, holding Carrie. He set Carrie down as she came up to him.

Laughing, Janie threw her arms around his neck, hugging him for all she was worth.

"You did it, didn't you?" she whispered in his ear, the angel-hair tickling her face. Happy tears threatened. "You told them about the cut-paper ornaments and talked them into selling them."

She kissed his cheek and stepped back, her hands still on those broad, muscular shoulders. Their eyes met and held.

"I told them," he admitted. "But it's your talent that'll make them sell."

"You can't know how much this means to me," she murmured. The tears spilled over and trickled down her cheeks. He pulled her close, holding her tenderly against his chest.

"Of course, I know," he said, his voice rumbling in his chest beneath her cheek. "I'm Santa."

Two days later, Filmore's launched the artist-in-residence studio and gallery with the fanfare of a theatrical opening night. Local celebrities, including Nick Klaus, attended the after-hours reception at the

Downtown Filmore's store hosted by a beaming Fil Filmore, owner and CEO of the Filmore Corporation.

Janie stood by the huge tree she had decorated with white lights and scherenschnitte ornaments. Her cheeks ached from smiling but at least that took her mind off the borrowed shoes pinching her toes. If only something could take her mind off the fear that no one would like her work!

"It's going great, Janie."

Nick Klaus had slipped around behind the Christmas tree to stand with her. She'd noticed how he stayed away from the reporters with their cameras and microphones. It didn't seem possible. Nick Klaus? Avoiding the public eye?

And why was he here, anyway?

Nick nodded toward the man standing before the TV cameras, being interviewed for the ten o'clock news. "Look at Uncle Fil, being the center of attention. You'd never know he has a phobia about being around people."

"You're related to Mr. Filmore?" Janie couldn't keep the disbelief from her voice.

"He's my mother's brother. He looks out for me. You see, my family is from Illinois, but I ended up playing football here in Dallas. Uncle Fil's the only family I have around."

"That's nice." She tried to sound as if she couldn't care less, but his information made her thoughts whirl. *That's* how he knew her. He must've been lurking in Filmore's and targeted her for some reason. Had he been stalking her? Misgiving squeezed her heart. She'd let this man into her home. He'd met her daughter. Before her anxiety could explode into accusation, she noticed how his expression appeared so lost, so forlorn, she almost felt sorry for him.

"It is nice," he agreed. "I don't depend on family ties that much, but Uncle Fil has stood by me during some rough times. In fact, I'll be working here after the first of the year."

Giving him a polite smile, she turned her eyes to the crowd, although her thoughts stayed on the man beside her. She admired his loyalty to his uncle—who must be a saint to stand by him through his mishaps—but why would he want to work in a department store? In spite of her determination to keep him at arm's length—farther, if she could manage it—she found herself intrigued.

"Why would you want a job at Filmore's?" she asked.

Nick shrugged. "My probation stipulates that I must be gainfully employed. The TV studio fired me."

Janie turned, looking him fully in the face for the first time. She noticed the arrogance she'd always seen in him on TV had disappeared. The famous blue eyes had no mischievous twinkle, no enticing smile touched his lips or brought out the dimple in his left cheek. He looked weary. "You mean they fired you because—"

"Because I pleaded guilty of a felony DUI and endangerment. That girl I was with almost died." He clipped out the words, avoiding her gaze.

Before she could respond, Mr. Filmore drew close, cameras in tow, including them in his speech.

"We're happy to introduce our new artist-in-residence studio here at Downtown Filmore's." Mr. Filmore gestured for Janie to stand beside him. Joining him, she hoped the soft material of her sweater and skirt hadn't wrinkled, and that her hair looked good. Gloria, standing to one side with Carrie, gave her a discreet thumbs up.

Mr. Filmore continued, "It is our goal to encourage talented young artists such as Ms. Langston by providing them with a studio and gallery to create and display their artwork. We hope to foster several artists throughout the year."

Applause greeted the announcement. Once the cameras were turned off, the crowd scattered to sample the buffet table and look at Janie's artwork.

While answering questions about the scherenschnitte ornaments, Janie saw a flash of red out of the corner of her eye. Her heartbeat quickened, and she turned in time to see Carrie running up to Santa. When the little girl got close enough to look into the man's face, she halted and put her finger in her mouth, then turned back to Gloria, who picked her up. Janie recognized Mr. Hopkins and understood Carrie's disappointment.

Since her meeting with Mr. Filmore, she'd been so busy designing the studio and making ornaments that she hadn't even talked with Santa. When she saw him it was merely to smile or wave in passing. She'd hoped he'd be here at the party so she could share the night with him in some way. After all, if it hadn't been for him showing the ornament to Mr. Filmore, none of this would've happened.

He could be here, Janie thought, gazing around the room. All the employees had been invited to the gala. If he was here but not in costume, how would she know him?

Gloria brought Carrie to Janie. The little girl cuddled into her mother's arms and laid her head on her shoulder.

"Are you sleepy?" Janie asked. "Are you ready for Gloria to take you home?"

"It's not bedtime yet, is it?" Nick asked, coming up from the shadow of the Christmas tree. Carrie's face lit up and she held her arms out to Nick.

Nick said, "If it's all right with you, I can take her to get some cookies."

"Thanks, but I'm sure you've got better things to do. Here, sweetie, go with Gloria." Janie tried to pass her off to Gloria.

Carrie squirmed in her grasp. "Down. I want him."

"Ahem." Janie looked at Gloria, who had discreetly cleared her throat. "I think it's time you introduced me, don't you?"

Janie's mouth fell open. First her daughter threw a fit over Nick, now her best friend was acting gaga. Was she the only female in the world immune to his charm?

"Nick Klaus, I'd like you to meet my roommate, Gloria Morton. Gloria, this is Nick Klaus." Carrie's wiggling made the introduction sound huffy. At least that was the excuse Janie mentally made for her lack of graciousness.

Nick shook Gloria's hand with a friendly smile but his attention was completely on Carrie.

"May I take her to look at the toys?" he asked, with such pleading Janie's heart melted.

"I can go with you," Gloria put in, cinching Janie's decision.

The instant Carrie's feet touched the floor, she scampered to Nick and hugged him around his knees. Reaching down, he took her hand. They headed to the toy department, ignoring Gloria.

"I'm losing my touch," Gloria lamented. "He'd rather be with a four-year-old than get to know me."

Janie watched them with an eagle eye, but it was hard to stay perturbed when she saw how Nick made Carrie laugh at the antics he created with the stuffed animals. "Maybe he likes younger women," she teased.

"My dear, the girl he had with him in that accident was ten years younger than he is," a woman remarked, overhearing the last part of Janie's comment. Although her skin had the crepe-like softness of an elderly woman, her hair was coal-black, pulled into a severe knot. Her eyebrows had been painted on, and her cheeks were generously rouged. Pursing her red lips, she held her glasses on the end of her nose as she looked at the painted greeting cards on display.

"His family's disowned him, except for the Filmore side, that is. And why Fil Filmore would risk his good

standing by taking on such a wastrel, I don't understand."
With a sniff, she dropped her glasses to hang around her
neck on a jeweled chain. "I'm an old friend of the family's, you see. That boy is the black sheep of the whole
bunch. You should be careful of him." With that warning, the woman swept off. Gloria and Janie watched her
slither through the crowd, dropping venomous words
along the way.

"Gee, with friends like that . . ." Gloria said.

Guilt flooded Janie's heart. The woman had said
aloud many of the things she had thought about Nick
Klaus. Except, look at him with Carrie.

Nick had carried her to the buffet table, where Mr.
Hopkins and Mrs. Coleman as Santa and Mrs. Claus
were holding court with the media. Carrie wanted nothing to do with the older Santa, she had her eye on some
decorated cookies.

"What do you want for Christmas?" Nick overheard
Mr. Hopkins ask Carmen Musgrave, one of Nick's for-
mer colleagues at the TV station.

"Well, if we were on-camera, I'd have to say something profound, like world peace," Carmen responded.
"But what I'd really like are some chocolate-covered
strawberries like these." She helped herself from the buffet table. "These are my secret sin."

Mr. Hopkins shook his head, then turned to Jeff
Stewart, the other news anchor. "How about you, young
man?"

"Ditto on the world peace. It's what the world needs

now. What *I* need are some new lures for fly-fishing. The ones I order from the specialty catalog are expensive. My wife lets me have it if I order too often."

Both members of the news team left the buffet without acknowledging Nick. He watched them go, thinking of their answers and what he'd have answered if anyone had asked him.

He was as shallow as anybody. The glib answers would've rolled off his tongue at one time. Now, without the glare of publicity blinding him, he'd seen some real needs, like the kids at the medical center. Or the homeless shelter where he'd gone, dressed as Santa, for some more community service. What he wished was for every kid to be as happy, healthy, and loved as the one he held in his arms.

He glanced up and saw Janie chatting with some people interested in her ornaments. Beautiful as always, discussing her artwork gave her an added spark.

His Christmas wish might be for the children of the world but his heart's desire stood before him. He wanted to hold both Janie and Carrie in his arms and in his heart forever.

Chapter Eight

Ignoring the milling crowd, Nick let Carrie lead him to a child-size table in the children's department next to Santa-Land. He balanced on a miniature chair, sharing the sweets arranged on the table with Carrie and two teddy bears, unaware of Janie watching his every move.

This wasn't the media darling, the bad boy broadcaster whom everyone indulged. When he looked at Carrie, his face relaxed and lost the bitter lines. Glancing up, Nick met Janie's eyes and lifted his cup of punch in salute.

Gloria waved a hand in front of Janie's face as she stared at Nick and Carrie.

"Hate to break this to you but you have some business. Ooh, wait, who's that?"

A man knelt at the table beside Nick and Carrie.

Mother's instincts aroused at seeing Carrie surrounded by strangers, Janie's smile evaporated.

"I've never seen him before," she said.

"He's gorgeous," Gloria breathed. "He looks like that guy on my favorite soap opera. Think Nick will introduce me?"

"You're fickle." Although he did look like the actor Gloria referred to, Janie didn't think he was all that cute. Indeed, his long narrow face, shadowed with dark stubble, couldn't begin to compare with, well, with Nick's clean-cut good looks, for instance. The other man's dark hair was on the longish side, complete with uncontrollable cowlicks. Nick's ruddy hair was carefully groomed. His blue suit fit in such a way as to complement the broad shoulders and muscular physique. It also brought out the blue in his eyes. The other man looked rumpled. Janie turned to tell Gloria so but she had slipped away, going over to the two men.

At least she'll keep an eye on Carrie, Janie thought with a sigh. She turned back to her work, visiting with guests and signing ornaments.

"What are you doing here?" Nick demanded when his agent pulled up a chair at the table with him and Carrie.

Unable to bend his long legs to sit in the miniature chair, Stan gave up and hovered.

Like a vulture, Nick thought.

"Thought I'd see for myself what Nick Klaus is up to

these days." He nodded as he looked around the room. "This is good, Nick, good. Get your name in with the artsy crowd, the conservative group."

"That's not what this is about. I'm not here to promote myself."

"Hey, whenever you're out in public, you're promoting yourself. That's why I'm here, to make sure you get good coverage. It's been hard to get in touch with you, lately. Where've you been, anyway? In disguise?"

Carrie put down her cup of punch. "This is his gusdize."

Stan looked as amazed as if one of the stuffed bears had talked.

"What is she saying?" he asked Nick.

Used to having people listen to her, Carrie climbed onto Nick's lap and stood on his good knee to put her closer to Stan's face. "This is Santa's gus-dize," she said. "He told me so." With that, she wrapped her arms around Nick's neck.

"You're Santa?" Stan laughed. "You?"

"I work here at Filmore's, yes," Nick said, wishing the guy would quit cackling. "And I'm going to stay on here at Filmore's after Christmas, working for my uncle. So I don't need an agent anymore." He stood, holding Carrie.

"No, no, no, you're not getting rid of me that quick." Stan twirled his fingers on either side of his head. "The wheels are turning, man. See, we've got to turn your image around. This Santa thing could do it."

Heat surged up the back of Nick's neck. "Stan—"

"Excuse me." Both men turned and looked at Gloria. She smiled, oh, so sweetly. "Is Carrie finished with her snack? It's getting close to her bedtime, you know. Oh, I'm sorry, did I interrupt?"

"Not at all," Nick said, glad for a break from Stan's machinations.

Stan seemed glad too, as he gazed at Gloria, taking in everything from her chin-length blond hair to the hint of toe-cleavage in her red-patent high-heels. "Nick, introduce me to the mother of this exquisite child."

Gloria laughed. "Oh, she's not mine. I just babysit sometimes."

"Gloria, this is Stan Wingate. Stan, Gloria Morton."

Taking her hand, Stan led her toward the buffet table. "Please, let me get you some punch."

Neither remembered Carrie, who cuddled in Nick's arms with her head on his shoulder, and yawned like a kitten.

In a store like Filmore's there was a dearth of comfortable places to sit. Nick didn't think he could bend his bad knee to sit in the little chair again. The best chairs were in Janie's new studio. He headed that way, admiring the renovations.

It had been decided to put the gallery on the third floor, which until now had contained the children's, housewares, and seasonal departments. Mr. Filmore and his managers had done a brutal cut through housewares, sending much of the merchandise to the mall stores.

They'd done the same with the children's department, leaving only specialty and collectible items in the downtown store. When Fil Filmore went exclusive, he did it big time.

The gallery area was carpeted, with the Christmas tree dominating the center. Track lighting shone on the tree and on the easels featuring Janie's hand-painted Christmas cards. The studio was set beside the gallery. Its floors were tiled, and it was outfitted with movable work islands and other equipment to meet the needs of the artists who would work there.

Supervising the setting up of the studio and gallery was quickly accomplished, but stocking it was a whole other thing. The cut-paper ornaments couldn't be mass produced. The simplest ones took a quarter of an hour to complete. Others, more complicated in design, could take hours. True to his promise, Mr. Filmore had provided several reams of paper in silver, gold, cream, and white. Nick had watched Janie working for the last couple of days, leaving a trail of snipped paper wherever she went. The response to the scherenschnitte ornaments was huge. Already, the tree was beginning to show bare branches where ornaments had been removed.

The Christmas cards would've sold, too, but Janie refused to put a price on them. Each card had been painted with the recipient in mind, and Janie couldn't imagine them going to anyone other than those for whom they'd been painted. Still, they had been well-received, with one person comparing the miniature portraits to Norman Rockwell's paintings.

Nick found a chair in the studio where he could hold Carrie and watch Janie without being disturbed.

The night was a triumph for Filmore's and for Janie. She never would have imagined how the exposure could launch her life in a whole new direction. People asked if she could be commissioned to paint portraits and murals. It was mind-boggling, going from being an unknown picture-taking elf to being a sought-after artist. She wished Santa, if he was here, would make himself known so she could give him proper credit for his role in making her dream come true.

Although the crowd wound down, Janie felt her nerves stretching thinner with each passing moment. She tried to remember the names of everyone she'd talked to, hoping she hadn't promised too much. She needed to be more organized than this. She needed business cards, an order book, a price list.

She needed to sit down.

Looking for a chair, she saw Nick with Carrie, sitting in the shadows of the studio, both sound asleep.

"Oh," she breathed. What a sweet picture. Carrie slept on Nick's shoulder, her finger in her mouth, the image of innocence. And Nick . . .

Seeing him with his cheek pressed against Carrie's curls made it hard to believe he was the hard-living scapegrace everyone made him out to be. In her childish innocence, could Carrie see more to Nick Klaus than his public image?

Flipping open her sketchbook, Janie drew a rough outline of the pair.

Nick's eyes opened and focused on her watching him. For a moment, they gazed at each other over the child's head, silently assessing.

She felt no threat from him; that had come from projecting her anger and fear on to him. Nick wasn't to blame for her problems, no matter how much he resembled her ex-husband. He had been nothing but kindness to her, protecting her, offering his help when he knew she needed it. He'd apologized to her, but she hadn't allowed herself to accept it.

Looking down at her sketchbook, she concentrated on filling in the small details of their features while she tried to figure out her feelings. In spite of Nick's kindness to her and Carrie, she'd reacted to him as if he'd attacked her rather than protected her. Or maybe overreacted was the better word. Like the "family friend," she'd been willing to believe the worst about him and act on that belief, even though he'd done nothing to merit her hostility.

He stood and brought Carrie to her. As he shifted the little one into her arms he gave her the sweetest smile she'd ever seen. For a man so large and with such strength, he was amazingly gentle.

"Thanks for looking after her," she said, then paused,

gathering her nerve. "And thanks for helping me before. At the bar. You've been very kind."

He nodded. "My pleasure."

Gazing up at his face, she felt an odd sense of recognition, as if she knew him. Well, why wouldn't she? Every night at 10:25 she'd watched him broadcast the news while pretending to be reading. Stealing another glance at his face, she couldn't shake the feeling that there was more to this impression of familiarity than just watching him on TV.

Boy, she must be tired, having fantasies like this. She stepped away and swept the area with a glance.

"It looks like everything's winding down," she said. "Hardly anyone is left. I wonder where Gloria is?"

"I introduced her to my agent," Nick said, nodding toward the couple in deep conversation by the buffet table. "Looks like they hit it off."

Mr. Filmore walked up and placed a hand on Janie's shoulder. "Congratulations, my dear. Everyone here at Filmore's is proud of you." Taking a large handkerchief from his pocket, he wiped it over his gleaming head. "This crowd has done me in. I need some peace and quiet."

"Oh, Mr. Filmore, there you are." Mrs. Coleman swept up all rosy-cheeked, two plates of food from the buffet in her hands. "I noticed you hadn't eaten anything tonight. I put a plate together for you."

Mr. Filmore's head turned pink. "Ah, thank you, Mrs. Coleman." He glanced at the young people and cleared his throat. "See you tomorrow. Congratulations again, Miss Langston." He took Mrs. Coleman's elbow in a courtly gesture and led her toward the back offices.

Janie turned to Nick, shifting Carrie's sleep-heavy body on her hip. "Thanks again. For everything."

Nick smiled and stroked Carrie's hair gently so as not to waken her. "Can I walk you to your car?"

"You don't have to do that," Janie said. "Gloria can help me—" She broke off as Gloria and Stan approached.

Gloria came up, an excited smile lighting her face. "Stan and I are going out for a cup of coffee. He'll bring me home later."

What could she say?

"Fine. I'll see you later."

As she watched the couple leave, the excitement and anxiety of the last few days overwhelmed her. Weariness struck, sapping all strength and energy from her body. She needed to get home.

"Janie?"

She turned to Nick. He said, "Let me help you take your things to the car."

"Thanks." She gazed around distractedly. "Everything can stay here, I guess. I just need to get my purse."

Nick helped her gather her belongings, then walked with her down the aisles of the store to the back and out into the parking garage.

"Do you want me to follow you home?" Nick asked after he helped her get Carrie in the car seat.

"No, that's all right. We'll be fine. Thanks for all your

help. Good night." She wouldn't linger but gave him a quick smile as she shut the door and drove off.

The private darkness and silence of her car allowed her emotions to pour out. She should be happy. Tonight she'd started living her dream of developing a career using her creative talents. So why was that overshadowed by disappointment that Santa hadn't been there for her big night? Wasn't she the one who always said she didn't need a man in her life?

She parked outside her apartment and got Carrie out of the car. Moving on autopilot, she put Carrie to bed, changed into some warm sweats, went to the kitchen, and made tea. It wasn't until she sat in the living room with the cup warming her hands that she let herself think.

Santa hadn't come to the party.

She'd thought he cared.

Her heart sank. She was such a fool. With guys like Nick Klaus or even Ryan, she knew she had to keep up the walls to keep from being hurt. But she'd thought Santa was safe.

The thought stopped her. Was that how she regarded Santa? Safe? Because of the costume, he didn't seem threatening, like real guys? Oh, but he was real, all man beneath the costume. She'd kissed him. What's more, the feelings she had for him went beyond friendship. If a day went by that she didn't see him, it was incomplete. And he'd done so much for her, going to Mr. Filmore with the scherenschnitte. But she didn't love Santa for the things he'd done for her or for his friendship, she loved him . . .

She loved Santa.

Goosebumps that had nothing to do with the temperature rose up all over her body.

She loved Santa!

Which meant . . .

What?

Nothing. It didn't mean he returned her feelings. If he did, he'd have been there tonight. He hadn't bothered to show up in costume or out.

Taking a deep shuddering breath, she let it out.

"Enough. I have everything I need. Carrie's healthy and happy. I have a fantastic new job and opportunities galore. What more could I want?"

Her resolve crumpled and she covered her face with her hands.

"I want someone to love me."

Sitting in Santa-Land the next day, Nick watched Elf Denise walk to the camera after helping a little boy onto his lap. The satin tunic hung like a shapeless sack on her ultra-slim body. Her stiletto-heeled, over-the-knee boots made her look like an alien Amazon from a sci-fi B movie. Or maybe a C or D movie.

Looking past Denise to Janie's studio, he rested his eyes on what he considered the epitome of an elf. She had smiled and waved when he walked past the studio to Santa-Land. Now she sat snipping at paper as if her life depended on it. He couldn't wait to get a chance to talk to her.

A flash of light distracted him, bringing him back to the job at hand.

"Did that picture turn out all right?" he asked, wondering what kind of expression had been on his face.

"It's fine," Denise assured him without even glancing at the monitor before hitting the print button. Coming toward them, she spoke in a syrupy voice. "And this little guy's such a good boy for sitting so nicely. Would you like a candy cane or a chocolate kiss?" She held out her hands, a candy cane in one and a chocolate drop in the other.

With her thick makeup and freaky costume, she was scarier than Big Mama Claus. The boy on Nick's lap shrank back against him, looking up into his face for reassurance.

"Take 'em both," Nick urged.

Grinning, the child reached out with both hands and grabbed his treats before sliding off Nick's lap and running to his mother.

"They're not supposed to do that." Denise watched the boy leave. "They're only supposed to get one treat."

"Then offer one treat," Nick said.

"But the other ones saw." Denise gestured to the line outside the ropes. "I'll have to give them all two treats."

"Yeah. Too bad. Better get the next one up here."

Nick gazed at Janie while Denise went for the next kid. If he'd known he'd wind up with a freaky elf, maybe he wouldn't have told Uncle Fil about Janie's talents. But it sure gave him a good feeling as he watched people come to the studio and buy those ornaments.

The whole store was busier today. With the shopping days 'til Christmas coming to an end, even Downtown Filmore's raked in the business. The big spread on the evening news the night before helped.

He talked with several kids while keeping an eye on the studio. When he noticed Janie had placed a BE BACK SOON sign, he took it as a sign to take a break too. Their own line had dwindled to one child. Nick finished talking with her, then told Denise, "It's time to feed the reindeer."

"Do what?" She looked at him, her red-lipsticked mouth pursed in a pout.

The girl had no sense of humor.

"Feed the reindeer, Elf Denise. I need a break."

Light dawned. "A break. Right." Switching to her sweetsy voice she announced, "We're going to feed the reindeer. Be back soon." A passing salesclerk rolled her eyes.

"Just put up the sign, Denise." Nick tried to keep the disgust out of his voice. He strode out of Santa-Land without waiting for her to catch up.

Luck was with him; Janie sat at the table in the break-room, eating her cup of yogurt. She glanced up at him as he entered.

"Hi, Janie."

"Hi." She tossed a smile in his direction and went on eating her yogurt.

Uh oh. She acted like she didn't want to talk to him. That had never happened before, not even when he'd pretended to be sick.

Proceed with caution.

He took the seat across from her. "How was your party last night?" he asked, knowing he had to be careful and conceal the fact he had been there.

"There were a lot of people. It was a very nice reception." She lowered her head, as if she had to give her full concentration to stirring her yogurt. "I hoped you'd be there."

It hit him all at once.

Duh.

She'd been looking for *him*. Santa. She had no clue her friend had seen her triumphant debut. It would've meant a lot to her to have him there.

If he'd been alone, he'd bang his forehead against the wall. He had such stupid, stupid luck. He'd been there the whole time, but because she didn't know he was Santa, she didn't know he'd been there . . .

Man, this was confusing.

He went to the refrigerator for his protein drink and tried to think through the whole Santa/Nick thing. Janie had seemed to warm up to him last night as himself. If he admitted he was Santa, would she understand and accept him? Or would his bad reputation wipe out the good he'd done as Santa?

Sheesh, what woman would want him? Even he knew he was bad news. But Janie had seemed to warm up to him last night, thanking him for helping her at the bar.

When he had stood with her and Carrie at the end of the reception, he'd wanted to put his arms around them both and hold them close. He'd been tempted to confess everything to Janie and ask her understanding. The moment had been lost when everyone else came up then went off two-by-two.

He needed to come clean with her. Even if it meant she would never talk to him again, he needed to tell her the truth. Leading her on, getting closer to her as Santa would be the worst thing that could happen. Somehow he had to find a way to tell her he and Nick were the same person. No more disguising his face or his heart.

Tell her now. Just open your mouth and tell her.

As he opened his mouth, a couple of clerks walked in the breakroom. Instead of confessing, he said, "Sorry I couldn't make it. Lots of calls for Santa these days."

No response. She wouldn't look at him.

"And there's so much to do," he went on, trying to connect with her again. "Making lists, checking them twice . . ."

That did it. She giggled, looking at him for the first time since he came in.

Maybe, if he was real smooth, he could change her opinion about Nick in these last few days before Christmas. She liked Santa. Trusted him. But Santa had to disappear after Christmas.

Elf Denise swept into the room, talking a mile a minute to an entourage of male clerks.

"She must've picked up every guy between Santa-Land and here," Nick whispered to Janie. "I don't see why."

Janie gave him a knowing look. "It's that stupid short tunic and all the makeup. And she's new here. The guys already know everyone else."

"Oh." Nick looked at the situation from a different perspective, remembering how he used to scope out new women on the scene. "Fresh meat."

Janie's cheeks grew red. "Right," she said, her voice filled with bitterness. "Fresh, easy meat." She slam-dunked her empty yogurt cup into the trash and headed out the door.

Nick followed, catching up to her in the corridor outside the breakroom.

"Janie, what's wrong?"

She sniffed and wiped at her cheeks, although he couldn't see any tears on them.

"Is that all guys see in a woman? Are they really only out for what they can get?"

"Some of them. But not everyone."

Regarding him a long moment, she took a deep breath and asked, "What about you? What do you want in a woman?"

"You."

The simple admission held them spellbound, in a bubble of privacy. He watched her lips curve into a tremulous smile, her face glowed. He knew—he knew!—she loved him.

Realization struck. She loved Santa. Not Nick.

This had to be settled. He couldn't go high to low to high like this, and he couldn't go another day without telling her the truth.

"Look, Janie, I really need to talk with you—"

"The reindeer are all fed, Santa." Denise sauntered over to them, batting her eyes. "Time to get back to work."

He was already on probation. Strangling a Goth elf would put him in prison. It might be worth it.

Janie touched his arm, reclaiming his attention.

"I get off work at five today," she said.

An invitation he couldn't accept, thanks to community service hours. "I have some volunteer work I'm doing this afternoon."

"Why don't you call me tonight?"

In spite of his anxiety in 'fessing up to his double life, his smile felt like it would bust the elastic holding his beard in place. "It's a date."

Chapter Nine

How was it that she got soaked giving Carrie a bath? The little girl wasn't overly rambunctious. Yet somehow, every evening, Carrie ended up clean and Janie ended up wet.

"How did my tennis shoes get wet?" she grumbled as she toweldried Carrie's hair.

"The bucket spilled, be-member?" As always, Carrie's thought processes filtered out any responsibility on her part.

"No more buckets in the bath," Janie said, more as a mental note to herself than to Carrie.

"Ouch!"

"Sorry, sweetie. I rubbed too hard. Here, stand still and let me comb your hair."

Carrie covered her head with her arms. "More owees."

"No, remember Aunt Gloria gave us this spray to take the tangles out?" Janie spritzed a bit in the air. "Mmm, it smells so pretty. Let me spray it on your hair, then it'll smell pretty too."

Carrie peeked out from between her arms.

The phone rang.

"Oh, drat," Janie muttered. "We'll just let it go to voicemail."

A second ring.

Carrie ran naked from the room. "I'll get it!"

"No, Carrie, wait." Janie hurried after her into the bedroom.

A third ring, and Janie remembered Santa's promise to call.

Not now. Her heart picked up speed as she rushed to catch the phone before the voicemail kicked in. *Not with my wet clothes and hair and Carrie running around naked.*

With a simultaneous leap and lunge, she threw herself across the bed, reaching the phone before Carrie did.

"Hello?" Her voice came out breathless, the result of her dash and vault.

"Hi, Janie? Have you been running a marathon?"

Santa. Her mouth went dry.

Carrie seized the opportunity to run into the living room.

"No, you don't," she said, starting after the child.

"I'm sorry?" Santa sounded confused.

That made both of them.

"Look, I'll have to call you back." Pocketing the phone, she dashed to find Carrie standing in front of the Christmas tree without a stitch on, her hair in damp tangles, dancing to the music of a TV commercial.

"You come in here right this minute." Grabbing Carrie's hand, she escorted her back to the bathroom where she spritzed the conditioner in her hair and yanked a nightie over her head. Carrie started whining and trying to get away. "Nope, none of that. We have to get your hair combed, then you can watch TV."

Janie marched into the living room with Carrie in one hand and a comb in the other. Settling herself on the sofa, she began combing at the knots in Carrie's hair.

"Ow, ow, ow!"

The phone rang. Janie pulled it from her pocket before it could ring again. Cradling the phone between her shoulder and her ear, she said, "Hello?"

"Is everything all right?" Santa asked.

Janie sighed. "Everything's fine. Carrie just finished her bath and I'm trying to comb the tangles out of her hair."

He laughed. "I remember when I was a kid, my sister wanted to get her hair buzzed like mine. She hated the tangles too."

"Long hair carries a price. Is your hair buzzed now?"

"What?" Once again, confusion from the other end of the line. Janie smiled to herself.

"I've never seen you without your costume. I know that long white hair isn't really yours. So, do you have long or short hair?"

"It's on the short side. I, uh, have a high forehead that seems to get higher every year, if you know what I mean."

"I see. And what color is your hair?" Finished with Carrie, she put the comb on the table and kissed the top of her head. Carrie took the comb and proceeded to comb BeBe's long ears while she watched TV.

Grabbing up a pad and pencil, Janie quickly sketched Santa's eyes and nose, then a high forehead with short hair.

"When I was a kid, I heard someone call it strawberry blond, so I never ate another strawberry. It's never been bright enough to be called a carrot top, but I made sure it wouldn't happen by boycotting carrots too."

Janie laughed. "You don't eat fruit and vegetables?" Unconsciously, she started sketching a fruit basket.

"Sure I do. Just not strawberries or carrots. What's your favorite food, besides yogurt?"

"Yogurt's not food, it's just something low fat and low-cal to eat."

His chuckle started a tingling in her toes.

"Why do you eat it so much?"

"It's like your high forehead, only on me, well, let's just say I'll never be as skinny as that new elf again."

"Man, I hope not. You're beautiful just the way you are."

Janie felt her cheeks heat up. "Thanks." Changing the subject, she said, "I would've called you back."

"What's my number?"

"Oh. Good point." How stupid could she be? "Even if I knew your number, I'd have to ask for Santa."

Silence on the other end.

Finally he said, "We need to talk about that."

"About you being Santa? I mean, you'd told me your name was Nicodemus but—"

"You thought I'd joke about that?" Again, he chuckled. "You can call me Nicodemus, I won't get mad. And I've noticed you sign your ornaments J-A-N-A-E. How about we call each other by our real names?"

"Even at work?" It didn't seem right somehow calling him anything but Santa at Filmore's.

"Mmm, good point. Okay. At Filmore's I'm Santa. But you're Janae."

"All right." Her drawing degenerated to doodles.

"Do you think we can get together tomorrow? I need to talk to you about . . . you know . . . after Christmas. I want things to be good between us."

Janie quit breathing, hope sprouting in her heart. He'd told her today she was all he wanted in a woman. Now he told her he wanted things to go on between them after Christmas. "Sure. I'll see if Gloria can pick up Carrie from daycare."

"All right."

Silence. Not complete silence. Janie could hear his breathing but she couldn't think of a thing to say.

"Is this a bad time to call?" Nick asked.

"No, it's fine, except I'll need to put Carrie to bed in a few minutes."

"Do you read her a bedtime story?"

Janie had never heard anyone smile before but she knew he was smiling. Her own lips turned up. "Yes, I read a story and get her a drink of water. Then I hear her prayers and get her another drink. Then, about fifteen minutes later, I have to help her go to the bathroom. Then she wants another story."

"What's her favorite story?"

"*Goodnight Moon,* by Margaret Wise Brown. She has a stuffed bunny that looks like the one in the book." Like he would know what she was talking about.

"Hey, I read that one this afternoon."

"You did?" Was there no end to the surprises this man had in store for her? She could almost believe he really was Santa Claus.

"Yeah. I did some volunteer work at Children's Medical Center this afternoon. The kids are real troopers and ready to have some fun. When the nurses said we couldn't play touch football, I ended up reading stories to them."

"You tried to play touch football in a hospital?" Janie wished she'd been there to see that.

"Like I said, the nurses said no."

Noticing Carrie asleep on the floor, she said, "I have to go."

"Time for that bedtime story?"

"No, too late for that. She fell asleep watching TV."

"Would you give her a kiss good night for me?"

She couldn't help smiling. He sounded so wistful, as if he wished he was there to kiss Carrie himself. "Sure."

"Can I call you again?"

"Yes, and I'll see you at the store tomorrow."

"Good night, Janae." Nick spoke in a whisper, making the salutation as intimate as a kiss.

"Good night." A moment passed before she hung up the phone, reluctant to cut off contact with him. Picking up Carrie, she took her into the bedroom and tucked her in the trundle bed. Kissing her forehead, she murmured, "Good night, little bunny."

"WHO IS THE MYSTERY SANTA?"

The headline screamed the question from the newspaper on Uncle Fil's desk. Nick had come straight to the office as soon as he saw it.

The article beneath the headline announced to the world that Downtown Filmore's had a new Santa whom no one had seen before. It went on to say that this same Santa had been spotted ringing bells for charity and visiting hospitals. Rumor had it—yeah, rumor, as in Stan leaked it to the press—that the Mystery Santa was a local celebrity turned philanthropist. And there it stopped, posing the question: Which local celebrity?

"I didn't do it," Uncle Fil said. "I hadn't realized no one knew who you were. Why haven't you told anyone?"

Nick sighed, running a hand over his face. "At first, I didn't tell the truth because I believed my own press. I thought I was too much of a big shot to be sitting in a store playing Santa to a bunch of snotty-nosed kids. I was embarrassed."

Fil tapped his pen on the desk. "You got over it. I've had lots of compliments on my young Santa."

"Yeah, I got over it." Thanks to people like Janie and Big Mama. Especially Janie. Nick leaned forward, his arms braced on his thighs, hands hanging loose. "What do I do now? This can't be good for Filmore's."

Uncle Fil's eyebrows shot up. "Between the art gallery and this, Downtown Filmore's has been in the news more than if I had hired a team of advertising consultants. The publicity's great."

Nick shook his head. "What I mean is, if I admit I'm Santa, it's going to be hard to make the transition to being your assistant. It looks like nepotism, like I didn't get the job on my own merits."

"Son, it *is* nepotism. This is a family-owned corporation. And while you had no experience or desire to be Santa, you've been successful at it." Fil waved a hand at the blueprints for the coming renovations. "Same with the business end. This was your idea, not mine. That's plenty of merit, if you ask me. I think it's time people start associating Nick Klaus with Filmore's and with good causes."

Nick shook his head again and stared at the carpet.

Fil regarded his dejected nephew a moment. "Why don't you tell me how all this secrecy began? I don't see how you've gone almost a month without anyone recognizing you."

Nick straightened. "The only people who know Santa is Nick Klaus are you and Ms. Garza. And I think Ms. Garza has forgotten."

"But don't you change into and out of your costume here at the store?"

"In the mornings, I get here just after opening. No one's in the back then, they're all out on the floor. Then, at closing, I just wait until everyone's gone."

Uncle Fil nodded. "Simple enough. Do you think you can keep doing that through Christmas?"

Nick raised his eyebrows. "What? Why?"

Fil leaned forward, resting his arms on his desk. "Because the papers have made it a big mystery. If you identify yourself now, or quit being Santa, it will reflect badly on Filmore's. But if you go along with it, we can milk this for all it's worth. I'll talk to Ms. Garza myself and make sure she's *forgotten* your name. All paperwork concerning you will be handled by me, personally."

"But people will be watching. All the time." When he had been in broadcasting, the thought of thousands to millions of people watching hadn't bothered him. In fact, it had inflated his ego to no end to be recognized wherever he went. But now he didn't want any part of the limelight.

His protests fell on deaf ears. Uncle Fil pulled over his ever-present legal pad and started scribbling on it. He said, "From now on, you're always in costume. When you arrive, when you leave, and at any public appearance involving Filmore's. And, my boy, there are going to be public appearances. You'll be Filmore's representative throughout the Dallas/Fort Worth area. You can change here, at my offices, and use the passage between buildings to get to work."

Nick nodded, an idea forming. He thought of ringing bells and the kids at the medical center. "All right. Like you said, from now on, I'm always in costume. If no one is supposed to know who I am, then that's how it's going to be. And not just as Filmore's representative. If I have to go through with this, we're going to use it to benefit other people."

Fil grinned, his pen poised above the paper. "What do you have in mind?"

Before leaving Uncle Fil's office, Nick changed into his costume and found his way through the passage between buildings.

Wait until he got his hands on Stan. This Mystery Santa deal was something else. It made sense, if you thought the same way as Stan Wingate. Any publicity is good publicity. All right. Stan's plan carried them this far. The plot he'd hatched with Uncle Fil would go even further, using the Mystery Santa to do some real good for the area charities. With any luck, no one would ever know Nick Klaus was the Mystery Santa, thus protecting Filmore's reputation without tainting it with his own infamy.

The hitch with this whole plan was he couldn't tell anyone his true identity until after Christmas. Not even Janie.

The passage ended in a door that opened into the office area of the store. Nick walked directly to Santa-Land without going downstairs to the employee lounge. As he passed the clerks, no one greeted him as they had before. Instead, everyone stared as hard as they could.

Wait until the new plan was in effect. They'd stare even harder.

"Santa, wait."

Janie's voice stopped him and he turned, waiting for her to catch up.

Hurrying to his side, she seemed to fizz with held-in laughter. Slipping her hand into the crook of his elbow, she whispered, "So I wasn't the only one who didn't know your name!"

"Make sure it stays that way, okay?" His spirits lifted at the sight of her, wearing a green sweater and a bead necklace Carrie must've made. Her merriment put a glow on her cheeks. He resisted the urge to kiss her nose. "Mr. Filmore and I have a great idea. We're going to use this Mystery Santa deal to do some good this Christmas."

"My lips are sealed. Is there any way I can help?"

They paused outside the studio. "Would you be willing to be my elf again for some special visits I'm going to make on behalf of Filmore's? You take much better pictures than Elf Denise. I know you don't like leaving Carrie," he said, seeing her hesitate. "It'd be all right if you brought her along."

"Fine. I'll be your elf again." She looked up at him, an enchanting combination of shy boldness in her smile. "I miss working with you."

His heart lurched. He wanted to work with her, to be with her every minute of every day. She wanted it too. But only as long as he was Santa.

He couldn't do this, couldn't keep her in the dark.

But he had to. He wasn't Nick Klaus hiding out anymore. He was the Mystery Santa.

"Listen, I have to break our date tonight," he said.

Some of her joy evaporated and she looked at him with a wariness that broke his heart. "Sure. That's all right."

Dropping his arm, she headed for the studio. He hurried to catch up with her.

"Janie, stop. Listen." He snagged her elbow, pulling her around to face him. "This Mystery Santa deal kind of took me by surprise. I have to deal with it, make the most of it for the charities. But it doesn't change how I feel about you. That's why I want you to work with me, because it wouldn't be right without you."

The glow came back to her face, melting the ice that'd built up around his heart when she walked away from him.

"It's all right," she repeated.

This time, it was.

That night, ten days before Christmas, Santa appeared on the evening news, challenging the people of the Metroplex to help him make this the merriest Christmas ever.

"I'll be happy to attend your Christmas parties, visit schools, hospitals, shelters, you name it, I'll be there," Santa said.

The colored lights twinkling in the Downtown Filmore's store windows made a bright backdrop. Fil Filmore himself stood in the background, beaming goodwill at all involved.

Santa continued his speech. "I'll be here at Filmore's every day until Christmas. You'll have plenty of opportunities to meet me and try to guess my name. I'll give you a hint—it's not Rumpelstiltskin." He grinned at the cameras, teeth flashing through the long white hair of his beard. "In order to be qualified to guess, send in a ten dollar donation to Mystery Santa, care of Filmore's Department Store. Part of the proceeds will go for an award to the person or persons with the correct guess. The rest will go to local charities."

Becoming serious, he braced his hands on the podium

and addressed the audience, the cameras zooming in for a close-up. "Let's have some fun this Christmas, and at the same time, remember those who are in need. Your donation means more than just a merry Christmas. It means caring and hope and help." His eyes became suddenly bright and he stepped back from the podium, waving with both hands.

"Wow," Gloria said, switching off the TV. She sat with Janie in their living room while Carrie played in the bedroom, giving the two women breathing space before fixing supper. "Can you believe it? You've been working with a mystery man since Thanksgiving."

Janie merely smiled and continued snipping ornaments. "It's just like him to find some way to help other people. I told him I'd help when I could. You know, go along and take pictures of kids with Santa so they'll have a gift for their parents. Mr. Filmore's providing a portable camera and printer setup." Getting up from the sofa, she asked, "What do you want to eat?"

Gloria also rose. "Nothing for me. I'm going out with Stan tonight."

"Again?" Janie grinned at her roommate. "How many times does that make, since the reception?"

Gloria beamed, happiness shining from her like a light. "I've lost count. Oh, Janie! He's the greatest guy. He treats me like a queen. I know he comes across kind of pushy sometimes but he's not like that, really. He cares about the people he represents as an agent. That's what he was doing at the reception—checking on Nick Klaus, making sure he was okay. Stan says Nick has been having a hard time lately."

Carrying a couple of apples and an orange to the counter, Janie started making a fruit salad. "He seemed kind of subdued at the reception."

Gloria snitched a slice of apple. "I swear he never took his eyes off you."

Janie shook her head. "I know I've been hard on Nick, and that was pretty unjustified. He's really a nice guy—"

"You don't know the half of it. Remember the girl in the car wreck?"

Janie nodded. Who could forget? If the girl had died, Nick would've been in prison for manslaughter. Thankfully, she'd recovered. Rumor had it she'd received a huge payoff to drop charges against Nick. Even so, he remained on probation.

"Stan said he was at the same party. He saw them leave. She was driving, not Nick."

Janie stared at her friend, paring knife poised in midair. "But everybody knows—"

"Everybody knows wrong." Gloria sat back, munching another apple slice. "Nick told Stan he took the girl from the party because she was in over her head. He was protecting her. Unfortunately, he didn't tell her no when she wanted to drive. The accident was her fault, not Nick's."

"That can't be true! Why would he . . . he lost his job because of this!" Even as she protested she knew it had to be the truth. From everything she'd seen of Nick, it was exactly the kind of thing he'd do.

Gloria went on. "According to Stan, Nick's been unhappy for a long time, like a midlife crisis or something. But lately, he's different. Maybe he needed a wake-up call, and the accident was it. Whatever. Stan says he'll do anything to help him."

"That's really great." And troubling. Gloria's story put Nick in a whole new light. It sounded so much like him—trying to help out someone in trouble, then have it backfire on him. Like when he helped her at the Honcho, and she got fired.

Gloria said, "I thought he'd call you, after the reception."

"I'm really not interested in Nick—"

"Because you've got it bad for Santa. Am I right?" Gloria grinned.

Why deny it? "He's done so much for me. I have a career now! I'm going to have a showing in an art gallery in February because of Santa. Me! It's unbelievable."

"And well-deserved." Getting up, Gloria headed for her room to change, calling over her shoulder, "But what happens after Christmas?"

Chapter Ten

At five o'clock the next day, Mr. Hopkins took over presiding in Santa-Land. Santa came to the studio and leaned on the counter. "Ready to go?" he asked.

"Ready." Janie put away her scissors and grabbed her purse. "I need to pick up Carrie, then we can meet you."

"I'll follow you to get Carrie, then you can follow me. I have all the camera equipment loaded in my car. And speaking of cars, wait 'til you get a load of what Mr. Filmore is making me drive."

As always, they fell into step as they left the sales floor on their way to the parking garage. Excitement— or maybe Christmas Spirit—bubbled in Janie's veins. The scherenschnitte ornaments were selling well, and she had three commissions for portraits to be done in the new year, as well as a showing at a local gallery.

Mr. Filmore had introduced her to the owner of the gallery. The owner not only was interested in Janie's work, but she also helped Janie develop a price guide for the portraits.

Then there was Santa. Stealing a glance at him, she smiled. He moved like a man on a mission, striding forward with purpose, in spite of his limp. He caught her eye on him and grinned.

"No more bah, humbug?" he asked.

She laughed. "Nope. From now on, I go about my days singing carols and waiting for Santa to visit."

It wasn't difficult to pick out Santa's car in the garage. A two-seated sports car, bright red, as befitted Santa's sleigh. Trimmed with silver and gold.

"Oh, my," Janie said, then pressed her fingers over her mouth to keep from laughing.

"Mr. Filmore's idea, not mine," Santa said, shaking his head. "He thought someone might run a license check on my car and discover my identity, so he made an arrangement with a friend of his—a car dealer—and here it is in all its glory."

"At least it won't be difficult to keep you in sight."

Their visit took them to a homeless shelter. Janie, Carrie, and Santa weren't the only ones visiting that night. Several reporters representing local news stations were also there. Although they tried to get up close and personal with Santa, they had to wait their turn. All the children wanted to talk to him, of course, and several of their parents. He listened to everyone.

Watching through the lens of the camera, Janie noted more changes in Santa.

Gone was the sense of boredom. He gave each person, child or adult, his complete attention. He didn't make promises or offer false hope. He simply heard their stories, sometimes motioning for a reporter to come and listen in.

"This is incredible human interest stuff," one reporter remarked to another.

"No kidding. And have you seen Santa's itinerary?" The man held out a sheet of paper that Santa had asked Janie to distribute to the reporters. "He's planning to be at church celebrations, hospitals, more shelters, nursing homes—"

"And a partridge in a pear tree," the first reporter said. "You'd think he'd worry about overexposure. Does he *want* people to recognize him?"

Janie stifled a laugh. For whatever reason, Santa didn't seem worried about being recognized.

A local celebrity, she mused. Imagine, she'd been working with a celebrity the last few weeks and hadn't known it.

Carrie ran up. "Look. Cookies! Want one?"

"Maybe later, sweetheart. I have to take pictures now."

" 'Kay." Her response was muffled by a mouthful of cookie.

Janie watched her, glad they had eaten a drive-through dinner before coming to help Santa. Although no one seemed to notice the photographer, everyone had fallen in love at first sight with the little angel who arrived on Santa's shoulder. After helping Santa lead a sing-along, she'd found many children to play with and was soon in the thick of the celebration.

Each person received a gift, courtesy of Downtown Filmore's Department Store. The gifts had been chosen with care—warm clothing for everyone, toys for the children.

The party wound down after a couple of hours. Janie packed up the camera equipment and located Carrie, who was sound asleep on an older lady's lap.

"Thank you," she said, leaning down to pick up the child.

"Thank you," the woman whispered, touching Janie's cheek. "And thank your man. He's too kind."

My man. She watched him circle the room, giving final greetings to everyone. When he arrived at her side, he put his hand on her waist and steered her toward the door. Not overbearing or possessive. Simply protective. Caring.

"Such a nice family," Janie overheard the woman say to the person sitting next to her.

"Good people," the man responded.

A family. Janie's eyes met Santa's. He gave her a smile and a nod that made warmth steal through her heart.

After they put Carrie in her car seat, Santa said, "I'll follow you home and make sure you get in all right."

At the apartment, Janie went ahead to turn on lamps and the nightlight while he carried Carrie to her bedroom and tucked her in.

"Did you have fun?" he asked, coming to the living room where Janie waited.

She nodded, then turned, drawing him with her to sit on the sofa. "I've never been to a homeless shelter before. Seeing the mothers with their little ones . . ." Her voice broke. "It could've been me and Carrie."

When he put his arms around her, she leaned against him, willing, for the first time, to share her worries. "If the artist-in-residence program hadn't come along, we probably would've been homeless. I couldn't pay rent. And I won't be a burden on anyone."

He stroked her cheek, his touch gentle, as if he wiped away the tears she shed alone, when no one could see. "A lot of people love you, Janae. Helping someone you love isn't a burden."

"But when I needed help . . . the person I thought loved me turned away." Tears came then, trickling down her face.

Cupping her face in his hands, he wiped a tear away with his thumb. "Then he didn't love you."

"And I was too stupid to know the difference." She pulled away from him.

He wouldn't let her push him away. He took her in his arms, cradling her head against his shoulder. "You're not stupid. You were young. I'll bet you loved him like crazy. *He* was the stupid one, not appreciating the love you gave him."

Sniffing, she sat up so she could look into his eyes. "Do you really think so?"

"I know so. Believe me, I know all about how self-centered a guy can be. But I've found out how much better life is when you start caring more about someone else than you do about yourself."

The expression in his eyes was completely serious.

"I love you, Janae." He put his forehead against hers. "I don't deserve you. I never will. But I love you with all my heart."

Happiness bubbled through her until she felt like it must shine from her like a light. "I love you too," she whispered. Raising her mouth to his, she kissed him.

She ignored the tickling of the angel hair, closing her eyes to blot out everything but the sensation of his lips on hers. Not just physical, although her heart rate quickened as she moved closer into his arms. The physical closeness was merely an extension of the caring they had for each other. Kissing him, holding him in her arms, being held by him, was . . .

Simple.

Natural.

Perfect.

"'Tchoo, 'tchoo!" The angel hair finally got to her, and she had to break away from him. Grabbing a tissue from the box on the coffee table, she rubbed at her nose, then settled back to her place in his arms. Twining some threads from his beard around her finger, she said, "This doesn't stay past Christmas, does it?"

He chuckled. "No way. Even I'm beginning to get

sick of it." He grew serious again. "Will you want me, even if I'm not dressed up as Santa?"

"It would still be you," she said slowly, mulling it over.

He lifted her chin with his finger, then brushed his fingers over her cheek. "No matter what I'm wearing, it will still be me, and I will feel the same about you."

"Well, son, it's the twenty-third. Not many more days until Christmas." Uncle Fil beamed at Nick as he came out of the executive washroom and stepped into the office.

"No, sir, it's not." It amused Nick that Uncle Fil, with two pet projects in his store, had taken to accompanying him when he walked from the office building to Santa-Land, like some incongruous bodyguard. He knew for a fact Uncle Fil had not spent as much time in the store since he had been a clerk working his way up to the main office.

The Mystery Santa had galvanized Downtown Filmore's. When Nick and Fil stepped onto the floor, clerks straightened and smiled as they passed by. Fil himself greeted each one by name, saving a special salutation for Doris Coleman.

"Good morning, Mrs. Coleman. I hope you're doing well."

Nick noticed Uncle Fil's bald head took on a rosy glow when he addressed Big Mama. She'd taken over picture-taking duties when Elf Denise, unable to keep up a cheerful facade, quit.

"Quite well, Mr. Filmore." Her eyes twinkled and cheeks grew pink, as befitted Mrs. Claus.

Nick hardly noticed the byplay between the older couple. His eyes sought and found the lovely Janae.

Stopping at the studio, he allowed Uncle Fil and Big Mama to go to Santa-Land ahead of him.

"Good morning," he said, drinking in the sight of her. She wore a sweater with glittering snowflakes scattered over it. But what truly sparkled and set his heart thudding in his chest was the emotion he saw in her eyes as she smiled at him.

"Good morning. Only two more days until Christmas."

"I know." It was hard to believe that in two days, this part of his life would be over.

In two days, the relationship with Janie might be over. Truth be told, Nick Klaus didn't deserve someone as wonderful as Janie. And Carrie—what kind of parent would he be? Not nearly good enough.

But in his heart, he heard Carrie's sweet voice saying, "Daddy." It sounded good. Right.

He could be a daddy. He loved Janie and Carrie with all his heart.

"What are the plans for tonight?" Janie asked, bringing his attention back to her.

"There's going to be a party for the kids at Children's Medical Center late this afternoon. You and Carrie up for it?"

Nodding, she said, "Why don't we let the kids make gifts for their parents? We'll take pictures, as usual, and

I have all kinds of craft stuff we can use to make frames or Christmas cards. I can even show the kids how to do scherenschnitte."

"That'd be great." Stepping closer and lowering his voice, he said, "Have I told you yet today how wonderful it is working with you?"

Her face glowed. "I think it's wonderful too." She caught her lower lip in her teeth, a worried expression on her face. "But I'm also scared. Having the gallery has been fabulous but it's almost over. And being with you, well, in a way, that's almost over too. I know I sound like a little kid but I don't want Christmas to end."

Nick gently chucked her chin with his fist. "You have to take it one day at a time," he said, calling up the words from his counseling sessions. "Today, we'll make a lot of kids happy."

Mr. Filmore joined them. "How will you make kids happy?"

Nick told him the plan. Once he grasped the idea, Fil waved off further explanations. "Be sure to bill Filmore's for whatever you need for those kids. In fact, could you use a couple of extra hands?"

Nick stared at his uncle. Where was the legendary shyness?

"We'd love to have your help, Mr. Filmore," Janie said.

His bald head gleaming, he scuffed his feet and said, "Well, Mrs. Coleman pointed out that no one wants a picture with anyone but the Mystery Santa, so we'll close down Santa-Land while you're at Children's Medical

Center. We thought it would be nice to go along, as the med center is one of the charities that will benefit from the Mystery Santa contest."

Nick threw his arm around the small man's shoulders. "That's great. Glad to have you with us. I'd better hurry to Santa-Land. Gotta get my hours in." And thank Big Mama for the transformation she'd worked on Uncle Fil.

Was this Christmas or what?

Janie paced the apartment as she waited for Santa to come by, pushed by the sense of unease that had haunted her all day. It *did* sound childish to wish Christmas would last forever but she couldn't help it. Actually, it wasn't Christmas she wanted to last as much as she wanted Santa to go on being Santa.

Tomorrow, on Christmas Eve, he would announce his identity to the world. He wouldn't be Santa anymore, just another guy dressed in a suit. Everything would change.

Huffing a sigh, she shook her head and scolded herself. *Oh, stop it. Nothing essential will change. Everything you love about him will still be there. His laugh. The way he talks to everyone as if they're important. His love for Carrie and for me.*

And won't it be nice to kiss him without the stupid beard?

She paused and watched Carrie, who sat on the living room floor, playing with BeBe and some blocks.

What would this do to Carrie when her beloved Santa quit coming around? And if he didn't quit coming around, if their relationship continued after Christmas, would Carrie understand that Nicodemus wasn't actually Santa?

Janie went into her bedroom to check her new outfit in the mirror. Groaning, she turned from her reflection and went back to the living room.

"What is with you, girl?" Gloria came into the room, looking bright and cheerful. She had volunteered to come along, bringing brushes, combs, a curling iron, and a multitude of Christmas hair bows so the kids would look their best for their pictures.

Janie plopped onto the sofa. "Tomorrow is the last day for Santa."

That caught Carrie's attention. "What'cha mean, Mommy?"

How could she explain this to a four-year-old?

"Well, tomorrow is Christmas Eve. After tomorrow, Santa won't be at Filmore's Department Store anymore. I'm going to miss him a lot."

Carrie shook her head, a mirror image of Gloria doing the same thing, but without the expression of amused disgust.

"Santa will use his gus-dize," Carrie said.

Reaching out and pulling Carrie onto her lap, Janie asked, "His disguise? What do you mean, pumpkin?"

"So nobody knows he's Santa. 'Cause he's so famous."

"I see." It was as good an explanation as going back

to the North Pole. They had probably read a story about it at daycare. "Then I guess I won't have to miss him, will I?"

Gloria said, "Don't worry. You can't change tomorrow. Just have some faith that, no matter who he is, he'll still care for you. Just like you'll still care for him."

The doorbell rang. Janie set Carrie down and hurried to the door. A peek through the peephole showed her Santa. Taking a deep breath, she opened the door. "Hi."

Nick gazed at Janie, unable to dredge up words of greeting. This was no ordinary elf. Red was definitely her color, from her sweater to the toes of the high-heeled boots peeking out from the hem of her jeans. Although the jeans hid her world-class legs, the sparkling sweater she wore should've come with a BEWARE OF CURVES sign.

Then there was Carrie, bouncing up and down behind her mother, looking like a candy cane come to life in her red-and-white–striped pants and shirt.

The elf and the imp, Nick thought, then changed his mind as his eyes returned to Janie. Angels. Both of them, Christmas angels.

"Come in," Janie said, leading the way down the short hall into the living room. "Gloria's going to ride with us. She's meeting her date at the hospital. They said they'd like to help with the party. Gloria's a hairstylist, you know, and can help the kids look adorable for their pictures."

"Fine. Great idea." Nick responded as he followed her. Who cared? Just as long as Janie was with him.

"Sit down," she said. "I'll just be a minute."

Nick sat on the sofa while Janie disappeared into one of the bedrooms to make some last-minute adjustment to her outfit. Carrie crawled up beside him and threw her arms around his neck.

"I like your gus-dize better. These whiskers tickle," she told him when she released him.

"You know what, Carrie, I'm starting to like the disguise better too. What would you think if I gave up being Santa after Christmas?"

"Would you still be my friend?"

Nick nodded. "I'd like that, if it's all right with your mom."

"Mommy likes you too."

Before Nick could think of a way to pump more information from this inside source, Gloria and Janie burst into the room, giggling.

Nick stood to help Janie with her coat while she made introductions. "Santa, this is my roommate, Gloria. Glo, this is Santa."

Gloria laughed and stretched out her hand. "The Mystery Santa. I guess you don't go by any other name."

"Not until after Christmas," he said, remembering he'd met her at the opening of the gallery. Did she recognize him?

Relief flooded Nick as Gloria pulled on a jacket and picked up Carrie, saying, "All right, squirt, let's get to the car."

Nick led the way downstairs to the cars. Due to his probation, Nick couldn't have passengers in his car. He'd loaded the camera equipment into the Santa-mobile, leaving no room for passengers. Janie, Gloria, and Carrie had to ride in Janie's car. Although he wished he and Janie could ride together, he wasn't going to take any risks. Straight-arrow rule follower, that was Nick Klaus from now on. Anything and everything he could do to earn Janie's love and respect.

At the hospital, the children and their families were gathered in a playroom. A hush fell over the room when Santa and his friends entered, then the children erupted in squeals of delight. Nick found himself mobbed by little ones.

"Okay, all right, hey there, big boy." Nick returned hugs, shook hands, and eased his way toward the chair they had set up for him. Janie and Gloria took Carrie to one of the long tables and started setting out the art supplies they'd brought along to make cards for the pictures.

"You have a way with kids, there, Santa," Stan murmured as he walked by.

Nick stared at his agent. "What are you doing here?"

Stan winked. "Just keeping an eye on the Mystery Santa. Not a bad idea, was it? After Christmas, everyone will think of you as Saint Nick for sure."

Nick's heart dropped to his shoes. "It *was* you behind this whole thing."

Stan crossed his arms, self-satisfaction oozing from every pore. "Not the whole thing. You and your uncle were the ones who turned the idea around." Stan nodded toward the door, where Fil and Mrs. Coleman stood, watching the activities.

"I'm sure I fired you," Nick said.

Suddenly serious, Stan said, "Look, man. I feel responsible for you. A lot of that bad-boy image you had was just that—image. It wasn't you. I knew it. You knew it. But I played it up. It kept your name out front. But it also landed you in a lot of trouble. This is my way of making it up to you. Think of it as a free image makeover." Looking around the room, he spotted Gloria. "I see my date. Talk to you later, Santa."

Nick watched as Stan walked away, glad to have the man in his corner. But would he really be able to change his image?

He didn't have time to think about it. Janie had finished setting up the camera equipment. The children gathered around, and Nick did his Santa thing. As he held each child on his lap, they chattered away. Sometimes they asked for certain gifts, but for the most part they were happy to sit and talk. Not restricted by time and long lines as at the store, Janie got some great shots of each child. When the pictures were printed, Gloria and Stan led the kids to the table where Mrs. Coleman and Uncle Fil helped them create cards for their parents.

Finally, Nick lifted the last child onto his lap—Carrie. She had a cookie in each hand and a red punch mustache. Hugging her close, Nick thought his heart would break, it felt so full. He touched her little nose with the tip of his finger when she looked up at him.

"I know you're a good girl," he said. "What do you want for Christmas?"

In reply, she snuggled against him and yawned, her eyelids dropping closed. He held her and watched her sleep, feeling the fullness of his heart swelling a lump in his throat and blurring his vision with tears.

"Here's your picture," Janie said, showing him a photo of himself and Carrie. She had managed to catch all the tenderness of the moment.

"But these are supposed to be gifts for the parents," Nick said, forced to speak softly around the lump in his throat.

Their eyes met and held, questions unspoken. Janie broke the silence. "I made one for myself."

Taking the cookies from Carrie, Janie picked her up out of Nick's lap. He stood and stretched, then walked with her to the tables.

"Looks like this one bit the dust," Stan said, nodding to Carrie.

"I'll hold her, Janie. You and Santa go get some punch." Gloria held out her arms and Janie slid the sleeping child into them. Nick was amused to see how Stan bent over the two of them. It was a side of his agent he hadn't seen before, a more human side Nick appreciated.

"Gloria's made a conquest," he said.

"She met him at the artist-in-residence opening at Fillmore's," Janie responded.

And he'd introduced them! *Whoa, this territory is get-*

ting complicated. Changing the subject, he remarked, "The party went well, didn't it?"

"Yes, it did." Looking around the room at the busy children, she asked, "Why are you doing this?"

"Doing what?" Nick gave up looking for a straw and put his cup of punch back on the table. No way was he going to get that red stuff against his white beard.

Making a gesture that encompassed the room, she said, "Are you here because you want to be here or because you have to be here?"

No easy answer for that question. Thinking it through, Nick answered slowly. "The first time I came here I thought it was because I had to. But once I got here and started talking to the kids I realized I wanted to be here. For them. Because this is the only way I can help them. Other guys are doctors or scientists. I'm not."

Smiling up at him, Janie reached out and took his hand. "You're better than a doctor or a scientist. You're Santa."

He should've felt on top of the world, with the warmth of her hand in his, but her words chilled his heart. Yeah, now he was Santa. Today, he could come here or anywhere else and put a smile on someone's face, maybe help them forget their troubles. But in less than twenty-four hours he'd put away the suit forever. Would Janie still look at him this way, as if he was some kind of hero?

Chapter Eleven

T wilight had fallen by the time they left the hospital. Gloria and Stan took off on their own for some last-minute shopping, leaving Santa to follow Janie and Carrie home.

Carrie fell asleep as soon as Janie strapped her into the car seat, and slept through the drive home. Santa took her inside and tucked her into bed, then came to the living room and sat with Janie.

"So. That's the last event for the Mystery Santa," she said, nervousness fluttering in her stomach. Their last date. Tomorrow his identity would be revealed and . . . what? Life would go on? Back to normal? What was normal?

"That was the last one," he said. "Didn't I tell you those kids are great?"

169

"They were great. And so are their parents. I would be a basket case if anything happened to Carrie."

"Not you," he said, reaching out and stroking a curl off her forehead. "You're a strong woman, Janae."

It must be magnetic force pulling her toward him, until their bodies touched, side to side, brown eyes gazing into green. She felt his breathing, the warmth of his arm curving around her shoulders, drawing her closer still.

As he lowered his lips to hers, the beard began tickling her nose.

I will not sneeze. I . . . will . . . not . . .

"'Tchoo!" Janie sniffed and rubbed her nose. She wanted so much to kiss this man. Not Santa. Nicodemus. The man who had made her dreams come true. Turning to him, she looked into his eyes, a determined set to her chin.

"I think it's time we get rid of this," she said, reaching for the elastic loops that held his beard in place. Sliding her finger behind his ear, she lifted the elastic free. He sat frozen before her, watching her as if he both feared and desired the revelation.

One loop free. Hardly daring to breath, she reached for the other loop—

"Mommy!"

Janie leaped up, every motherly instinct on alert, Santa rising beside her.

"M-o-m-m-y!" Carrie cried, gagging at the end of the word.

They moved together, flying down the short hallway to Carrie.

The child was so sick to her stomach, she didn't question why Santa was still there. Instead, the poor thing clung to Janie, crying.

Nick stood, helpless, while Janie crooned to Carrie. Every time Carrie retched, Nick turned away and swallowed hard. How could Janie sit there without getting sick herself? Finally, when the sickness passed, Janie picked up Carrie and took her into the bathroom.

Feeling like he was intruding, Nick backed out of the room into the hallway.

What a night. If Carrie hadn't gotten sick, who knew what would've happened? Probably Janie would've removed his beard, and *she* would've gotten sick.

He wasn't ready for this. It was probably his fault Carrie got sick. They'd taken her among so many people, so many germs.

These last several days, he'd gotten caught up in the Santa thing, as if he really was the old guy. As if making some public appearances dressed as Santa and giving money to charities would make up for his past and make him worthy of Janie's and Carrie's love.

The best thing he could do for both of them was leave. Get out of their lives before he screwed things up even more.

Stepping to the door of the bedroom, he heard Janie's voice over Carrie's pitiful crying.

"It's all right, sweetie. I'm here and Santa's here. We'll take care of you."

Nick closed his eyes and made it a prayer. *Let me take care of them. Both of them. Forever.*

Opening his eyes, he saw the room from a new perspective. Come what may, he was here for Janie and for Carrie.

Peeking into the bathroom, he saw Janie wiping Carrie's face with a washcloth. All right. Janie had Carrie under control. Now he had to do his part to take care of the situation.

But what?

Turning away from the bathroom, he couldn't help but notice Carrie's bed. *Eeuw.* Parenthood was not for the faint-hearted or the weak-stomached. Something had to be done about the soiled bedding.

Nick was the only one around to do it.

Yechh.

Gingerly, he pulled the corners of the sheets free of the mattress and tossed them toward the center of the bed, making a large bundle of sheets, blanket, and everything else on the bed. As he picked it up—what was that line? Like a peddler just opening his sack, only this one was going to stay closed—Janie and Carrie emerged from the bathroom.

Carrie was wearing a clean nightie but looked pale and weak.

"Here, Carrie, you can stay in Mommy's bed tonight." Janie tucked her into the big bed.

"I want BeBe," Carrie said.

Janie looked at Nick. He looked at her.

"What's a BeBe?" he asked.

"A stuffed bunny."

Nick shook his head. "It . . . um . . . it's so . . ."

Turning back to Carrie, Janie told her, "BeBe needs a bath. When she's all clean I'll bring her to you."

Carrie sniffed and snuggled under the covers.

"What do you want me to do with these sheets?" Nick asked.

Janie took the sheets from him and put them in a plastic laundry basket. "Is BeBe in here too?" she asked.

Nick nodded.

"Then I'll take everything to the laundry room." Janie carried the basket into the hallway. "If you don't mind waiting here with Carrie."

"I'll wait," Nick said, then, "Wait! Where's the laundry room?"

Janie nodded toward the door. "It's in the courtyard by the pool. It'll just take me a minute to get this going—"

"I'll take it." Nick came up and took the basket from her. When she opened her mouth to protest, he said, "I'd feel better if you stayed here and let me wash the sheets. I think Carrie would too."

The line of tension between her eyes relaxed. "Thank you. Everything you need is in the basket."

Gazing into her eyes, he said, "Everything I need is right here." His throat closed up, he couldn't say anything more. With a nod of promise, he turned and left the apartment.

Janie went back into the bedroom to finish cleaning up.

She tried to work quietly, to give Carrie a chance to sleep, but Carrie was wide awake.

"Mommy?" She peeked at Janie over the top of the quilt.

"Do you need something, sweetie?"

"Can I have a drink of water?"

"Sure." Janie fetched some water in Carrie's favorite Peter Rabbit cup, watched her sip it, then set it on the bedside table. "How does your tummy feel?"

"It's all right."

Janie went to the linen closet and returned. As she struggled getting the fitted sheet over the mattress on the trundle bed, she heard, "Mommy?"

"What, Carrie?"

"I love Santa."

"I do too," Janie whispered before she had a chance to think about it.

"He wants to be friends when Christmas is gone."

"That's nice. But you don't need to worry about that right now."

"I like his gus-dize better."

Janie gave up on trying to get the fitted sheet to fit and sat on the edge of the bed. "His what?"

"His gus-dize. When he doesn't look like Santa."

"Oh, his disguise. Well, I guess so." *What isn't to like?*

Broad shoulders, gorgeous eyes. "But he's not Santa, then."

Carrie yawned. "He's just the same," she said, snuggling into the blankets. In seconds, she was fast asleep.

How simple, Janie thought as she watched her daughter sleep. *No matter what he looks like or what his name is, he's just the same. Always Santa.*

In memory, he stood before her, saying *Everything I need is here.*

He'd looked at her as if making a vow. He loved her, she was sure of it.

She loved him. True love that lasted through every season. Very shortly, Christmas would become Christmas Past. But the changes Santa had brought to her life would continue.

As would her love for him.

Nick prowled among the washers and dryers in the deserted laundry room. Cold air filtered through cracks where the caulking had fallen from the windows. The door wouldn't close due to some problem with the hinges. He paced, doing laps around the island of washers to keep warm.

Lifting the lid on the washer, he peered in, wondering if he'd loaded the thing right. The agitation stopped, and the clothes sat in a tub full of dirty, sudsy water, smelling strongly of chlorine. The bleach bottle said it killed germs and disinfected, which seemed like a good idea, so he'd poured a generous dollop on top of the sheets before turning on the washer.

Nick wondered why the washer had stopped. It wasn't finished by a long shot. Jiggling the coin slot didn't help. Thinking he'd try pushing and pulling the knobs on the washer, he lowered the lid back into place and—*voila!*—the machine worked.

Cool.

Nick opened and closed the lid a few times, amusing himself with finding just the right amount of open it had to be before it quit working. Then the thing went into spin, and Nick backed away from it.

And bumped into reality.

Well, it was the wall, but it was as hard as reality.

He loved Janie and she didn't love him. She loved Santa Claus.

Nick shook his head. This kind of thinking was too much for him. He wasn't used to defining his feelings. He worked great on instinct, without thinking things through. Well, not always so great. The alcohol had messed up a lot of his better instincts but now he was sober. He was out of the limelight.

Thing was, he wasn't sure who he was anymore. Looking back on the events leading up to the disastrous party and accident, he realized he had just gone through motions, like an actor playing a part. He didn't get involved. No emotional attachments. He just plain didn't care.

But the accident and subsequent sobriety made him

care. He couldn't get away from the responsibility for what he'd done. The newspapers had settled down. All that was left to do was wait out the terms of his sentence.

What he hadn't counted on was being changed by his sentence. When he looked back on his life, he wasn't proud of any of it. The exploits on the football field were over and done with. He couldn't live on that fading glory for the rest of his life. That was then. Who was he now?

He went to the window and looked out over the court-yard surrounded by the apartment building. Not many lights were on in the apartments, making it easy to pick out Janie's place. He stared at the glow that shone through the drapes, imagining Janie as she tended her sick child.

Sobriety made him realize that his life had no purpose whatsoever. None. Zip. Nada.

That's what he liked about being Santa. He had a mission to help other people. He understood why Janie liked Santa better than Nick. He did too.

The washer quit running with a final jerk. Nick pulled the sheets out and stuffed them into a dryer. He hoped they were clean. They looked kind of funny . . . tie-dyed or something. He hadn't noticed that when he brought them in, but then, he'd been busy trying to keep his supper down.

He had no idea how long it would take for the sheets to dry, so he decided to check on his girls.

His girls. He liked the sound of that. Uncle Fil and

Mrs. Coleman often mentioned what a cute trio they were, and people regularly mistook them for a family. What he wouldn't give for that! But it had to wait for the Mystery Santa contest to end. They could start fresh, after Christmas.

Would Janie give him that fresh start? She'd made it clear she wanted nothing to do with Nick Klaus. To-night, before Carrie got sick, when Janie started to re-move his beard, he hadn't known whether to stop her or rip it off himself. Pausing at the foot of the steps, Nick looked up at the door and reached a decision. He would tell Janie tonight—take off the beard, reveal himself for who he was. This was going to be either the best or worst Christmas of his life.

When he reached the landing, he was startled to see Janie at the door of the apartment holding Carrie as she tried one-handed to find her keys in her purse. "Thank God you're here," she said. "Carrie's running a high fever, and I'm so scared. I'm going to take her to the emergency room."

"I'll drive." Grabbing the keys from her hand, he led the way downstairs. Once they got Carrie fastened into the car seat, they took off, Nick driving, and Janie in the back with Carrie.

Going thirty miles an hour over the speed limit, beat-ing cars through the intersection as the lights changed, and passing on the right side had been much easier when he was too drunk to care. Now he cared too much, about everything. He cared about the little girl who cried in the seat behind him. He cared for her mother. He cared for himself.

Feeling sorry for the kids at Children's Medical Center hadn't prepared him for what he felt now, with a sick child of his own.

She wasn't his own.

Yes, she was. Blinking back tears, he peered through the windshield, the knowledge blooming in his heart. She was his because he loved her and because he loved Janie.

Flashing lights in the rearview. Now *he* felt sick. This could change his sentence from probation to prison. Once the officer saw his license—

"The police are behind us," Janie said. "They want us to stop."

"I'm not stopping until we get to the hospital. When we get there, Janie, you take Carrie in. Don't worry about me."

"All right." At her subdued tone, Nick risked a glance back at her. She regarded him with eyes round with concern and glittering on the verge of tears.

Nothing he could do about it now, he thought, punching the accelerator to squeeze through a stale yellow light, the police on his tail.

They swung into the emergency room parking lot, Nick and Janie getting out of the car at the same time.

"Don't worry about me," Nick repeated, watching the officers emerge from their car. Taking his attention from them, he placed his hands on Janie's shoulders. "Remember, no matter what, I love you."

Tears tracked down Janie's cheeks. "I love you too." She kissed his cheek and disappeared through the hospital doors.

Nick turned and watched the officers approach. Their displeasure at being led on a high-speed chase showed in their faces as they moved into the light.

"Look who we have here," one said, giving Nick and his Santa suit the once over.

"Now I've seen it all," his partner chimed in.

I can explain.

Nick was tempted to offer his excuses, starting with those three words. How many times had he uttered them, then managed to talk his way out of trouble?

No more. No more excuses, no more shirking responsibility or consequences for his actions.

"I take it you were speeding because of an emergency," the first officer said.

Nick saw he wasn't without sympathy. "My friend's daughter is sick. I brought them to the hospital."

The officer nodded. "I'll need to see your license and registration."

The moment of truth had arrived. Nick reached for his wallet, knowing the minute the officer saw his name, his freedom would be taken away. If he had it all to do over again, he would've done the same thing. He'd risk his life for Carrie or Janie.

"Wait." The second officer shined a flashlight directly in Nick's face. Turning to his partner, he said, "You know who this is? It's the Mystery Santa."

Peering at Nick, he said, "Yeah, it is." A grin spread over his features. "Just in time for me to check your license and get my guess turned in."

"That's just it," his partner hissed. "We can't bust Santa. Some of that money's been promised to the police department. If we run him in and publish his identity, how much do you think the department's going to see?"

Nick had sense enough to keep quiet.

"If I let him get away with these violations, what kind of cop am I?" the first officer demanded.

"It's Christmas. His girlfriend's baby is sick. Give him a warning. But don't look at his license."

The other officer nodded, all hesitation gone. "I'm not even gonna write this up. It never happened. It'd better not happen again."

"No, sir," Nick said.

Both officers went back to their car, leaving Nick standing on the sidewalk. He heaved a deep sigh, looked up into the starry night, and said, "Thanks."

When he found his way to the ER waiting room, Janie and Carrie weren't there. That was a good thing, he told himself. It meant the little girl was getting the medical help she needed.

After an hour of shifting around trying to sit comfortably in the molded plastic chair, he got up and approached the person sitting at the reception desk.

"Ms. Langston and Carrie are with the doctor now," he informed Nick. "It shouldn't be much longer."

"Thanks." To his relief, Janie and Carrie came through

the doors from the inner sanctum before he had to sit again.

"Is she all right?" he asked Janie, peering at Carrie's face.

"She's fine. The doctor said there's some virus going around that causes upset stomach and high fever. The fever's already gone down. I guess I just overreacted. I'm sorry."

Putting his arms around both of them, he hugged them close. "Don't be sorry. Just be glad everything's all right."

Janie rested her head against his shoulder. He could feel the weariness of her body as it trembled against his.

"Let's go home," he whispered, and kissed the top of her head.

He drove them home, following every traffic rule and signal. After they returned to the apartment and got Carrie settled in bed, Nick remembered the laundry and went to fetch it from the dryer. Now he wished he was facing the police again. He'd turn himself in on the spot if they'd just show up. Anything rather than standing before Janie's wrath.

"You bleached BeBe?"

The stuffed bunny hung limp in Janie's hand, looking like, well, like a bleached bunny.

"What am I going to do?" Janie demanded, holding the bunny toward him.

"You think she'll notice?" Nick asked, without any

hope. Of course, Carrie would notice. *Anyone* would notice.

Janie didn't reply, just gave him a hard look, then pulled the sheets out of the basket.

They were definitely tie-dyed. From Janie's expression, Nick gathered they hadn't started that way.

"The bleach bottle said it killed germs. I didn't know it—"

"Bleaches?" Janie interrupted. She put the sheets back in the basket. "You've never done laundry before, have you?"

"No. Not recently, anyway." Nick waited for her to yell at him to get out but she didn't. She sighed, her shoulders sagging, as if pushed beyond endurance. "I was trying to help, Janie. You needed to stay with Carrie. I messed up your sheets and BeBe. I'll buy you new ones."

Janie flipped a hand at the sheets. "These will be fine. But BeBe's another matter. She was handmade, by my grandmother."

"Could she make another one?"

"She passed away two years ago."

"Guess not," Nick muttered under his breath. He needed a Plan B. Plan BeBe, to be exact. "Let me take BeBe. If she misses it—"

"Oh, she'll miss it," Janie assured him.

"Tell her Santa took it. I'll see what I can do about getting it fixed up and bring it back before Christmas."

Her annoyance evaporated. "If you can get BeBe fixed by then, you really are Santa."

"Only until tomorrow. After that—"

"After that, it doesn't matter what you call yourself. I know who you are—the man I love." Standing on her tiptoes, she placed a kiss on his mouth. "Good night, Nicodemus."

He tucked BeBe under his arm then, laying his finger under her chin, gave her a kiss like a promise.

"I'll be back, Janae," he said, and disappeared into the night.

She stood a moment, leaning against the closed door, weariness dragging at her body. Finally, she picked up the basket of laundry and took it to the living room. She shook out the sheets and folded them, grimacing at the irregular white splotches decorating them. What a mess. And BeBe—he'd have to be the real Santa Claus to fix BeBe.

Sighing, she put the sheets away in the linen closet, then peeked at Carrie from the door of the bedroom. The little one was sleeping, holding on to a stuffed bear in lieu of BeBe. The doctor had said as long as the fever stayed down she would have a full recovery in time for Christmas.

Leaving the sleeping child, she got a blanket out of the linen closet, went into the living room, and stretched out on the couch. Closing her eyes, she consciously relaxed her muscles, letting the tension unwind from her body.

She hadn't meant to get mad at Santa when he brought in the sheets. But after the fear and helplessness she felt when Carrie got sick and the ordeal of going to the emergency room, seeing the ruined bunny had been the last straw. As good as it had felt to vent her emotions, he didn't deserve her going off at him after all he'd done for her.

Poor guy. He hadn't told her about dealing with the police, but it must've been bad enough without her yelling at him to top it off.

With her eyes closed, she pictured him in the parking lot at the emergency room. She had shivered, more with anxiety than cold. He looked over her head at the approaching officers, then at her.

Remember, no matter what, I love you.

No matter what.

No matter that she panicked when her child got sick, no matter that he bleached the sheets, no matter that BeBe was ruined. Somehow, it would all work out because not only did he love her, she loved him.

Tomorrow she and the entire Dallas/Fort Worth area would know his name and what he looked like.

He'll be the same, she reminded herself. Still, the thought niggled at her brain. What did he look like, under the beard?

Suddenly restless, she swung her legs off the couch and sat up. At times like this she turned to drawing, letting random images flow from her brain to her sketchpad until she felt peace in her heart and mind. Picking up her sketchbook, she flipped through it and found a clean page.

Santa. Everything came back to him. It only made sense to draw his portrait.

Smiling, she recalled the image of Santa holding a sleeping Carrie. The rough sketch took shape on the pad. Tilting her head, she studied it.

She'd seen this picture before.

Sure. The photo she'd taken. She gave one to Santa and kept one.

No. That wasn't quite the same.

Nibbling on her bottom lip, she dotted the paper with the tip of the pencil while trying to remember just what made the picture seem so familiar. She'd seen this before, but where?

Flipping through the other pages in the sketchbook, she stopped when she came to the rough sketch she'd drawn at the artist-in-residence reception of Nick Klaus sitting with Carrie, both sound asleep.

It can't be.

The pictures were almost identical. Carrie was the same, of course, but Santa and Nick . . .

The same tilt of the head. Same posture, with the left leg stretched out.

It can't be!

Snatching up the sketchbook, she flipped over the pages to a blank sheet and started a new sketch. Just Nick's face—the eyes, crinkling at the corners when he grinned. The square jaw.

Then she drew over the picture, adding Santa's hat, beard and hair. As she worked, memories came to her. Santa, walking with a slight limp. Nick Klaus, with the bum knee that took him out of football. His strength, lifting kids on and off his lap.

Oh, no, no, no. There's no way. Santa—*her* Santa—couldn't be Nick Klaus.

She drew, making broader and broader strokes, the pencil grooving into the paper until it tore.

Ripping the paper from the book, she crumpled it and threw it across the room.

Then retrieved it from where it rolled under the TV.

Spreading it out on the coffee table, she gazed at the two faces, one beloved, one despised.

"I've done it," she whispered. "I've fallen for Nick Klaus."

Chapter Twelve

The sound of a key turning in the lock of the apartment door drew her attention away from gazing at the two drawings. She looked up in time to see Gloria giving Stan a last good-night kiss before coming into the apartment.

Quickly, she tucked the pictures into her sketchbook and closed it, tossing it onto the coffee table. Gloria glanced over on the way to her bedroom and noticed her sitting on the couch.

"Hi," she said, detouring into the living room. "What are you doing up?"

Janie's thoughts scrambled, trying to think of what to say. "Carrie's sick," she blurted. "I thought she'd sleep better if I stayed out of the room."

"That's too bad." Gloria tossed her coat onto the armchair, then came and sat on the other end of the couch, tucking her legs under the blanket. "I hope she feels better for Christmas."

Janie nodded. "The doctor said she should. It's just a virus. Mostly, we have to make sure she doesn't get dehydrated."

Gloria looked at the clock, which showed just past midnight. "When did you take her to the doctor?"

"We had to go to the emergency room."

"Oh, no." Reaching across the couch, she patted Janie's hand. "You should've called. Stan would've brought me home, and I could've helped."

"It's okay. Ni—I mean, Santa was here. He helped me through everything." Janie was glad she'd caught her slip of the tongue before saying Nick's name. Now that she'd realized Nick and Santa were the same, she no longer thought of them separately. Nick was Santa, Santa was Nick.

But Santa's identity was supposed to be a mystery to everyone. She couldn't slip up now and give him away.

Gloria didn't appear to notice the blunder. "Santa's a great guy."

"He's incredible." Janie picked up her sketchbook and hugged it.

"Are you still worried about what will happen with him after Christmas?"

Janie remembered how Nick had looked at her in the parking lot at the hospital, the promises he'd made there and here, after they'd brought Carrie home. In spite of the suspicion she'd treated him with every time she'd met him face-to-face out of costume, he'd helped her beyond measure. She had told him tonight she loved him, no matter what.

She was a woman of her word.

"No worries at all," she said.

High noon on Christmas Eve. Apartment-bound with Carrie, Janie sat in front of the TV watching the Mystery Santa news conference. The cameras showed Mr. Filmore locking the main doors, signaling that Filmore's was closed for Christmas. Santa appeared on the scene, bounding onto the stage set up outside Downtown Filmore's, his enthusiasm overcoming his limp.

Janie's breath caught at the sight of him. Scanning his face, she couldn't believe she hadn't recognized Nick, even under the beard. Had anyone guessed Santa's identity?

Accompanied by Mr. Filmore, Santa waved a warm greeting to the people gathered on the scene. Carmen Musgrave and Jeff Stewart were on hand from Channel Thirty-two News as emcees.

Santa braced his hands on either side of the podium and spoke into the microphones. "I want to thank everyone who participated in the Mystery Santa contest. It's my pleasure to announce that the winner is . . ." Turning to Mr. Filmore, he held out his hand, waiting to be given an envelope. Mr. Filmore beckoned for him to step closer, then whispered in his ear. Santa listened, nodded, then returned to the microphone. "The winner is Children's

Medical Center, the United Way, the Salvation Army—"
His voice was temporarily drowned out by feedback from
the public address system and from the stir in the crowd.
He held up both hands, motioning for the crowd to quiet
down while the sound technician made some adjustment.
When the feedback ceased, Santa stepped back up to the
mike.

"The winners are the charities. A total of eighty thou-
sand dollars will be divided between them. You see, no
one guessed my alter ego. But I'll tell you." He leaned toward the mike as if imparting a secret. The crowd unconsciously shifted toward him. "I'll tell you," he repeated.
"Christmas is a time of mystery, of doing good, of sharing with others." He turned to Carmen and extended a
wrapped package to her. "It's remembering that someone's favorite treat is chocolate-covered strawberries." He
handed a similar package to Stewart. "Or that their hobby
is fly-fishing." Both commentators took their packages
with stunned expressions.

Santa continued. "I'm proud to have been a part of
your Christmas this year and look forward to Christmas
in the years to come. There's still work to be done, and
I will continue throughout the year with the good work
we've started this Christmas. I might not wear the suit
but I'll still be Santa. See you next year." With that, he
waved and left the stage with the applause of the crowd
following him.

The two commentators appeared on-screen, dressed
in their Christmas best, with disconcerted expressions.

"This is a Thirty-two exclusive," Jeff said, recovering his professionalism. "Although the announcement wasn't what we expected, the crowd seems to appreciate it." Indeed, the people gathered around the stage appeared especially joyous as they shook Santa's hand and wished him a Merry Christmas. "What do you think, Carmen?"

Musgrave had a wistful expression as she clutched her box of chocolates. "I think I believe in Santa Claus."

The screen blurred and Janie realized she had tears in her eyes. "I believe in Nick Klaus," she whispered.

An hour later, the doorbell rang. Janie peeked out the peephole then opened the door. "Santa?"

"Hi, Janae. It's . . . me."

As always, the sound of his voice brought warmth to her heart. Why had she never recognized Nick's voice as Santa's? Love wasn't only blind but deaf as well.

"I know," she said. "I mean, I know who you are."

But it was obvious who he was. Dressed in the complete Santa costume, he looked the same as he had every day since she'd started working with him.

"I need to talk to you," he said. "But first, how's Carrie?"

"Carrie's fine. She's had a little fever but not as bad as last night. She was awake earlier this morning. She's been having a nice long nap since then." She automatically led him down the hall to the living room.

Santa—Nick—put a couple of packages under the Christmas tree before sitting beside her on the sofa.

"You said you know who I am." He raised his eyebrows, making it a question.

She nodded. "Last night, after we got home from the hospital, I made some sketches and realized who you really are." She gave a laugh. "I feel so stupid. I never figured it out."

"No one figured it out. It's crazy. I took on the Santa gig so I could hide. Then something happened . . . I met you and Carrie . . . and I wanted to be Santa. Not ho, ho, ho, and all that, but someone you could love, who you can trust."

He sat back, his grin radiating through the angel-hair beard. "Then, when the results of the contest came in, that no one recognized Nick Klaus as the Mystery Santa, I decided I'm going to keep on being Santa."

"You mean . . . the hair, the beard . . ."

"Yep, the whole thing. Maybe not the red velvet suit all the time. Uncle Fil has given me the title of Director of Philanthropic Activities for the Filmore Corporation. Sounds like a job made for Santa. Like I said this morning, the good deeds need to keep on all year long."

"You said you'd be watching. You wouldn't wear the suit." It was just too bizarre. He couldn't be serious. She caught his mood, at once playful and serious, and listened to him avidly as he outlined his plan.

"Hey, I'm not totally dumb. I noticed how people treated Santa, how much everyone loves him. Why would I want to give that up? Especially if it's what keeps you and me together." He took her hands. "That's all I want for Christmas and every day for the rest of my life, for us to be together. If I have to be Santa to make it happen, then that's what I'll do."

Janie squeezed his hands. "Nick . . . Nicodemus. You've been so wonderful to me. Because of you, I have a chance to make a living through my art. That's more than I ever dreamed." Tears ran down her face and emotion choked her voice. "You've been a wonderful friend. Carrie loves you." Her voice faltered, she hung her head. "I love you too. But can you forgive me? I believed every bad thing anyone said about you."

He took her in his arms, letting her hide her face against his shoulder. He spoke, his voice strong, wonderful, reassuring. "I know it seems like every time I'm around you, something bad happens. That kills me, because I only want the best for you. I know *I'm* not the best. The only good thing in my life has been being with you and Carrie."

Sniffing, she wiped her eyes and sat back so she could see his face.

The tenderness in his eyes matched the emotion that made his voice suddenly husky. "Janie, I love you. These last couple of weeks of being with you and Carrie every day have been the best of my life."

Before she could respond, Carrie appeared at the bedroom door, her face crumpled. "Where's my BeBe?"

They both turned toward the child. She trudged into the living room and unhesitatingly leaned against Nick's knee. He drew her onto his lap, saying, "I had to take

BeBe to my house. I brought her back, in that package right there under the tree. BeBe has a surprise for you."

Carrie left Nick's lap and pulled the package from under the tree. She tore the paper with no method except to get it off in the quickest possible way. The lid flew through the air, and Nick blessed the reflexes that allowed him to catch it before it hit anything breakable.

Carrie gazed into the box, her mouth open in surprise. Reaching into the box, she pulled out *two* stuffed bunnies—one white, one brown. The white one was dressed in a long white dress and held a bouquet of flowers. The brown bunny was also elegantly dressed in a tuxedo, with a flower in his lapel.

"BeBe is all white," Carrie said.

"That's because she's a bride," Nick explained. He picked up the brown bunny. "This lucky fellow here is her husband, Bobby Bunny."

"Oh, Mommy! BeBe got married." Carrie hugged the bunnies to her and danced with them.

Nick grinned at Janie.

"How did you find another BeBe so fast?" she whispered, leaning her head against his.

"I got it from Big Mama—I mean, Mrs. Coleman." Nick took her hand and squeezed it. "She's a great lady. She has several grandchildren and knows how to sew. I guessed she would know what to do about BeBe, so I called her first thing this morning, before the Mystery Santa announcement. She had another bunny already made but said Carrie would know the difference if we tried to substitute it. So she finished bleaching BeBe, dressed her up, and let me have the other bunny to explain the changes in BeBe."

"Wasn't it kind of drastic for her to get married?" Janie asked.

Nick grinned. "It's a big step, all right." He tweaked her nose. "You wouldn't want to do that with just any bunny."

Carrie climbed onto the sofa between them, holding the newlywed bunnies. Nick put his arm along the back of the couch and tugged at a stray wisp of Janie's hair. She returned the favor, pulling at the angel hair. They shared a smile over Carrie's head.

Nick had proven himself the opposite of everything she'd believed about him. It wasn't a surprise that no one guessed the Mystery Santa's identity. Even she, an artist, hadn't been able to recognize the physical likeness between the two men due to the differences in character she believed existed.

How much of Nick Klaus, bad boy broadcaster, had been hype?

Most of it, she decided. And she had fallen for the hype, hook, line, and sinker.

But now she'd fallen for the man.

Yet, he still seemed to believe he was the same man the tabloids wrote about. He, who had given so many people new hope and second chances, didn't believe he deserved the same for himself.

How can you get someone to believe in themselves?

He had done it for her. He'd listened and watched, and when an opportunity had arisen to help her, he had stepped forward. He believed in her.

All right. She believed in him. It was time to stand up for him as he'd stood up for her.

She pulled at the angel hair again. "It seems to me we got interrupted last night."

He raised his eyebrows, his expression wary. "Maybe that was a sign that we shouldn't mess with a good thing."

Slowly shaking her head, she said, "No. It's like those packages under the tree. The real gift is under the wrapping. The real guy I love is under this beard."

He caught her hand, keeping her from pulling the elastic loop over his ear. "Are you sure?"

"I'm sure." She reached up and took his cap and wig off, then gently removed the beard. She leaned over and placed a kiss on his lips. "This is so much better."

He sighed, his breath warm against her mouth. Then his arms came around her, pulling her close. "I love you, Janie." He kissed her, releasing the weeks of longing they'd both felt but hadn't been able to express.

"You're squishing me!" Carrie wiggled between them.

"Oh!" Janie hadn't thought about Carrie, about what seeing Santa without his beard would do to her, much less what seeing her mother kissing Santa would do. Would this irreversibly warp her little psyche?

No. The little girl stood up on the sofa, put her hands on either side of Nick's face, and gave him a smacking kiss of her own. "I like your gus-dize better than your beard," she said.

"Your gus—oh, my!" Janie laughed. "She's been talking about Santa in disguise for weeks. I thought she'd heard a story at daycare. She meant you."

Nick nodded and took her hand. "She's known ever since that first morning I came here and told her I worked with you at Filmore's."

Carrie climbed off the couch, still holding her bunnies. "I'm gonna show Bobby his new house," she said, going to her bedroom.

Alone at last. Janie gazed at Nick, who wiped the last bit of makeup out of his eyebrows with a tissue. How was it she hadn't recognized him? The odd thing was, she hadn't recognized Nick when he was in the Santa getup, but she saw Santa every time she looked at Nick's face.

Taking a deep breath, she looked him straight in the eye. "I am so sorry I judged you before I knew you. You've been nothing but kindness to me and Carrie. You've been more than kindness. You've been there for me throughout the last month. And I've done everything I could think of to push you away."

Nick stared at his hands, loosely clasped where they rested on his knees. "You pushed Nick away," he said. "But you've been a good friend to Santa."

"Nick and Santa are the same person."

"You didn't know that." He laughed. "You know, I

was jealous of myself. I noticed how people treated Santa, the characteristics they liked about him. So Nick started developing some of those characteristics."

Smiling, Janie said, "I think Nick had those characteristics all along." She leaned against his arm, nudging it until he put it around her. "After all, you took the blame for an accident that wasn't your fault."

"Janie—"

"Tell me about it. Please, Nick?" Reaching up, she laced her fingers through his, pulling his arm more snuggly around her shoulders.

He sat for a long moment without speaking, then let the story come out, halting, hurting.

"She was so young. It must've been her first time to party with the big dogs. She drank a lot, trying to keep up with everyone else, then got sick." He paused, breathing hard, as if he'd been running. "I was sick too. Of the party. Of the lifestyle. I realized that night that no matter how much I tried to pretend, I didn't belong there anymore. It was scary, not knowing where I fit in. So I decided to take the girl home."

"You rescued her from a bad situation," Janie said, her voice soft. "Just like you did with me."

"I'm no hero, Janie. Once we got away from the party, out in the fresh air, she felt better. She'd never driven a sports car before and wanted to drive mine. I let her. I didn't think she . . . I didn't think. Next thing I know she's hauling down the highway like we're in the Indy 500. Next thing after that, we're wrapped around a light pole."

"Why did you take the blame?"

"I thought she was dead. Everyone was going to blame me, anyway. I didn't see any use trying to get out of it. I knew I deserved whatever I got. She didn't. All she'd done was go to a party that was too much for her. The good thing is, she recovered. She's going to be fine. Live to party another day." He hoped to heaven she'd learned her lesson.

"How about you?"

"No more parties for me. No more alcohol or drugs. No more being a player of any kind. I've learned over the last month there are more important things in life than any of that."

This time, she didn't sneeze when he kissed her.

"This is much better without the beard," she murmured, stroking a finger along his jaw.

"Is it really? I mean, do you really love me, Nick Klaus? 'Cause I'll do whatever it takes if you'll love me even half as much as I love you."

"I love you, Nick Klaus."

He pulled her closer into his arms. "Will you still be my elf and help me keep the promises I've made?"

"Nope." She shook her head, the dimples appearing in her cheeks. Putting all her hopes and dreams on the line, she said, "I want to be Mrs. Klaus."

Epilogue

"Tell me again how you and Mommy fell in love and got married," Carrie said, watching Nick hang her stocking on the mantel.

"That was just last year, Carrie, and you were there for most of it," Nick said, smiling as he imagined the goodies he was going to place in the colorful stocking.

"BeBe and Bobby don't be-member. Tell us again." Carrie picked up her bunnies and brought them to the sofa, where she took her place between Janie and Nick.

Nick and Janie exchanged smiles over her head. Decorating their house for Christmas awakened memories for all of them. This had become Carrie's favorite story for the season.

"Once upon a time," Janie began.

Nick reached out and stroked her hair. "Santa fell in love with an elf."

"He's not really Santa, just one of Santa's helpers, 'cause he's a bilandrobist just like Santa," Carrie stage-whispered to the bunnies. "And Mommy's not really an elf, either. She's an artist."

Janie took up the story. "So they got married and the elf became Mrs. Klaus—"

"We be-tended it was Christmas in July for our wedding," Carrie chimed in. "And Santa 'dopted the elf's little girl. Then they moved into a big house next door to Uncle Fil and Aunt Doris."

Nick often teased his uncle about his December-May romance—that is, they'd met in December and married in May. He never teased Aunt Doris. In his heart, he was still a little afraid of Big Mama.

"But that left Aunt Glo all alone in her apartment," Carrie continued. "So, she and Uncle Stan got 'gaged. They're going to have a wedding in the middle of the night on New Year's Eve."

Nick reached across Carrie and took Janie's hand, joining them together as he concluded, "And they all lived happily every after."